The Pekinese Princess

In the far-distant Pekinese Kingdom there was an air of jubilation, for the Pekinese had won a great victory over their treacherous enemies, the monkeys. And now Amber Face, the bravest warrior among them, was to marry the beautiful princess, Stars in a Dark Pool.

But the vengeful monkeys were bent on destroying the celebrations of the Pekinese. Wang, the cleverest of them, crept into the kingdom disguised as a juggler. He kidnapped the princess and ferreted her away.

So began Amber Face's perilous search through sinister forests and rough mountain passes. With him travelled a gallant band of warriors, and the animals of the land – the cormorant, an ancient turtle, the spotted leopard and the green dragon gave their support. But it seemed that even the courage of the Pekinese and their friends would not be enough to withstand the cunning of the enemy.

THE
PEKINESE
PRINCESS

PAULINE CLARKE

Illustrated by Cecil Leslie

COLLINS
ARMADA LIONS

First published 1948 by Jonathan Cape Limited
First published in Armada Lions 1973
by William Collins Sons and Co Ltd
14 St James's Place, London SW1

© Text Pauline Clarke 1948
© Illustrations Cecil Leslie 1948

Printed in Great Britain
by Richard Clay (The Chaucer Press), Ltd
Bungay, Suffolk

Contents

1. The Princess

Far away beyond Samarkand, beyond Mongolia and beyond the great mountains and plateaux which separate these from China, there lived very long ago a little Pekinese Princess. She was small and tender beyond description, the most beautiful daughter of her father, the Emperor of the Pekinese Kingdom. Her colour was between gold and cream, her paws were fringed and as if dipped in snow, her face was as dark and soft as soot. But her chief beauty was her bright and luminous eyes, which twinkled like stars and glowed like fires. For this reason she was called Stars in a Dark Pool, and she was deeply loved by her father, the Emperor, and her mother, the Empress.

These two ruled in peace and friendship the kingdom of the Pekinese, which lay not very far from the great city of Pekin. The Emperor lived in a gorgeous palace of pale green jade and pearl, which stood by itself on a slope, surrounded by pine trees, prunus trees and maples. A rapid river, rushing down from the hills above, cascaded in a waterfall a short distance from the palace and then pursued its way, chuckling and chattering through the Emperor's gardens.

It was a fine day in springtime and a feeling of excitement

spread through the Pekinese kingdom. Bells and musical stones could be heard ringing in some of the temples, where the priests seemed to be busy preparing offerings. The Pekinese in the market place were extra talkative, and stood longer at each stall chatting to the shopkeepers. Some houses flew flags and long coloured banners from their verandas. The children were in the streets carrying lanterns and toys and were playing in groups instead of being occupied in school.

For, the fact was, that the Pekinese army was expected home after pursuing and defeating a band of murderous monkeys who had lately swept over the plains intending to capture the kingdom. The messengers had brought news that the victorious army was not far away; and this was the reason for the people's pleasure.

But while all this was going on, the Princess, Stars in a Dark Pool, was wandering round her own dear little island in the middle of the river which ran through the Imperial gardens, dreaming to herself among the almond trees and singing songs. And this was one of the songs she sang:

THE PRINCESS'S SONG

Petals on the almond tree
Lotus on the water
There was one the Dragons loved
The Emperor's sweet daughter.

Lone she lived and all alone
With her lonely laughter
Strung her tears on a silver chain
The Emperor's sweet daughter.

A million whispering willow leaves
Words and wisdom taught her,
Love she learned from silence,
The Emperor's sweet daughter.

By this song it appeared that the Princess was not very happy that day. She was tired of stitching fine silken garments and tiny silken shoes (she had made one pair with pavilions, in red, all round the heels) so she asked her maiden, the beautiful and favoured Pekinese, the red-gold lady Golden Bells, to play on her lute.

'Play loudly, Golden Bells, so that I can hear wherever I go,' said the Princess; and she went down to her willow tree which had been her friend ever since she was a baby princess, six inches long, and had lain beneath its branches. She called this tree Silver Sorrow because its arms drooped sadly towards the water.

'Silver Sorrow,' said the Princess, 'do you know what may happen today?'

The tree gathered its million pointed leaves together and shook them, answering, 'Tell me.'

Stars in a Dark Pool gazed into the river and said nothing for a moment.

'Will he come, or won't he come?' she sighed at last.

'He will come,' answered the willow.

So the Princess got up restlessly and hurried back to the scarlet pavilion, where Golden Bells sat sewing.

'Will you taste some swetmeats?' asked she, seeing her mistress; and she held out a little round box in the shape of a leaf, full of scented comfits and sugar fruits. The Princess shook her head.

'Alas,' said her maiden, 'you are very sad, to refuse comfits. Will you swing on your swing?'

The Princess waved her fan listlessly as she moved towards the swing, and Golden Bells laughed her soft golden laugh which was the reason for her name. Then she went on with the embroidery.

'There,' she said a little while later as she put in the last stitch, 'you have ten silken dresses with borders of silver and gold, ten pairs of satin shoes, ten coats with wide sleeves and dragons curling round them, ten beautiful sashes and tassels of different colours.' And she hung them all up neatly, folding the sashes in a little pile near the shoes.

'But what is the good,' sighed Stars in a Dark Pool, 'of all these things and no husband? What shall I do if he never returns from the land of the monkeys?'

'He will come,' said Golden Bells. 'The messengers said they might arrive today.'

'Supposing he is wounded?' said the Princess, 'supposing he does not recover?'

'O, suppose and suppose,' said her maiden, teasingly. 'But I think he will soon be here. When I have picked some almond blossom to stand in the hall, I shall go to the water's edge and see.'

'Oh no!' said the Princess quickly, 'it would not do for me to be expecting him.'

'Chopsticks!' said the maiden, and went into the pavilion. Stars in a Dark Pool stayed swinging, and looking out over

her father's kingdom. It was a fertile and happy country, where grew fruits and flowers of all kinds, luscious and delightful, where rivers and rocks sang, and the birds spoke from the trees to those who passed. It was protected from its enemies by a Great Wall, like the wall of China itself, but neither so large nor so long; and upon this wall the monkey hordes had swept down. Round the wall valiant guards were posted, square-jawed, waving their standards of pomp (sometimes called their tails) in the air. The guards on the west looked out over a rolling plain, and in the very misty distance, a wide river. More distant still towered the mountains; and what happened beyond these only the wayfarers among Pekinese could ever know, the fighters who went out to battle, or those who set out alone to find adventures in the solitude.

Inside the wall, all was peace and contentment. The streams were dotted with minute emerald green islands, and upon these the rich had their summer pavilions. On a hot day you would see them rowing across in their flat punt-like boats, while the willows drooped to the water and the fishes dived beneath the little bridges. Here, too, the white lotus flowers lay, and the green frogs sat delicately upon them, ready to leap and dive when the long-billed herons flopped down.

The Princess fixed her eyes on the mountains and sighed,

and imagined that she heard the faint sound of pipes and drums, and then the shrill noise of Pekinese cheering.

And, indeed, the army was at that moment entering the gates. A little band of the returned warriors, hurrying ahead of the rest, approached the Emperor's palace, still wearing the signs of battle and holding their standards of pomp high in the air.

Great consternation seized the old Official of the Emperor's household, as he saw the fierce band rocking along; for he was a little short-sighted and did not recognise them.

'You can go no further,' said the old man querulously from outside the wall of the palace where he had run, 'until you explain who you are and what brings you to the palace of the great Emperor, beloved of the green dragon, the guardian of our kingdom.'

'Nonsense,' replied the leader of the band (rather rudely, for he was young and high spirited, and in a hurry – which was no excuse for being rude). 'I am the son of the Emperor's oldest warrior, General Puffer, and have just returned from conquering the hordes of the monkeys.'

'If your courageous and militant Eminence will come a little nearer, I shall be able to see properly,' said the old Official, huffily, peering through his spectacles. And with a shuffle and a grunt, he led the little band past the guards and through

the pearl gateway. Here he turned and kow-towed (that is, he bowed, scraping a step or two backwards), and then set off at a shambling pace across the gardens and the courtyards towards the Emperor's summer palace.

The Emperor was the colour of the red bear and his face was massive and dusky as a forest at evening. His forelegs were as bent as a bull-frog's, and embroidered upon his rich yellow robe the green dragon sprawled. He sat on his summer throne of bamboo, and all round him blossomed almond and magnolia and other sweet flowers. As the warriors bowed before him, he rose to his feet, waved his Imperial paw and said:

'Rise up, O Pekinese warriors, whose jaws defend our king-

The young mandarin laying out the gifts

dom, and tell us from the beginning the tale of the defeat of the monkeys!'

So the General's son, whose name was Amber Face, stood up and told him stories of adventure and hardship, of pitched battles and pursuits; and of how the sacred bats flew in the faces of the monkeys to confuse them.

'And, O beloved Emperor, I have brought back the teeth of the monkeys to adorn your Imperial furniture, and their hair

to make mats for your halls,' finished the young Mandarin, laying the gifts out.

'So well have you done,' said the Emperor beaming, 'that your esteemed father and I have arranged a reward. You are to marry the most beautiful Pekinese in the land, Stars in a Dark Pool, my daughter, who is even at this moment preparing gifts and a rich dowry.'

The delighted Mandarin lay flat at the Emperor's feet, prostrate with excitement, his square jaw raised in thanks, and his standard of pomp quivering as he rolled from side to side. For he had once before seen the beautiful Princess as she played in the Imperial gardens with her maidens, and had loved her ever since. He dared to hope that she too loved him, because seeing him stare she had waved her little fan, made of the tail-feathers of a bird of paradise, and then had hidden her sooty face behind it.

'How soon may I see the Princess?' asked the Prince (or Nearly-a-Prince).

'As soon as you can walk to the Island of Almond Blossom, where the Princess and her maiden are waiting for you,' replied the kindly Emperor.

For in the Pekinese kingdom men and women met frequently as we do, unlike those in the rest of China, who lived cut off from each other – a dull and dreary existence.

2. The Monkeys

So, after kow-towing most humbly once more before the Emperor, Amber Face and his few followers set off in high spirits across the Imperial gardens to where the little river ran between its green banks studded with flowers and ferns. Here, two of the Mandarin's followers turned back, leaving him with his best friend, Chu-i, a captain who had been with him in all his battles. Then they stepped into two small boats, and toad attendants pushed off with their poles.

At this moment, as it happened, Golden Bells had crept down to the water without telling the Princess, to see if there were anybody coming. As she stood there, the boats which carried Amber Face and Chu-i came skimming between the lotus leaves from the other side.

'Quickly, quickly,' called Golden Bells, to her mistress. 'Two boats are coming across the water, and in them are two warriors!'

And the Princess scampered joyfully down to the edge just as the Mandarin's boat ground the shore.

Clasping her white hands, she bowed low and led the Mandarin up towards the scarlet pavilion, there to feast him on sweetmeats and tea from spring buds, while he told her of his adventures with the monkeys.

'What are the monkeys like?' asked Stars in a Dark Pool (for she had never seen one).

'Ugly and savage, without much fur, and with shiny black hands' (the two maidens shuddered with fright), 'and they swing along on the branches of the trees with their strong arms and legs,' said Chu-i, the red-coated.

'There was one in particular,' said the Mandarin, 'who

could jump further than all the rest. When I saw *him* coming I prayed to Buddha and thought of the sacred jewel flaming in the jade temple. You could tell him by the bent and crooked thumb on his left hand.'

'Have you killed them all?' asked Golden Bells, and she looked at the two warriors with admiration.

'A few ran away,' casually replied the young Mandarin, his flat nose turned towards the river.

'But we do not expect any more trouble from *them*,' added Chu-i. And the warrior and his friend sat blandly smiling, thinking how fortunate they were to be home once more after all their troubles, and how happy to be sitting with the Princess in her scarlet pavilion on the Island of Almond Blossom. How far away the dark forests seemed, how remote the evil monkeys!

Alas for the proud Pekinese, sitting securely on the island in their kingdom! Little did they imagine that far away in the dark monkey forest a small band of the enemy were gathered at that very moment, plotting revenge on the inhabitants of the happy kingdom. They sat in a close ring round their fire, and their shadows flickered and bobbed as the flames leapt up. For in the depths of the forest the light dies quickly, and the trees close in with the light as if they were stalking nearer. The monkeys had built their fire in a small clearing, bordered by great evergreen oaks and closed in with bushes. They had eaten their supper of nuts and roots and had fallen silent, thinking of the recent battles and their absent friends, killed by the Pekinese. The forest was full of little noises, crackles and footfalls, cries and chuckles, as birds and creatures flitted or crept through the dusk to their homes or their hunting. And still the monkeys sat hunched and gloomy staring into the fire.

'I should not mind so much,' said one ugly creature at last, 'if it had been the leopards or the tigers – but to be routed by the inconspicuous troops of the Pekinese, some scarcely out of the litter . . .' and he spat with disgust into the embers.

'They were thousands, and we were only hundreds, you forget,' said another monkey. His eyes glinted red in the firelight, and his teeth flashed.

'They had Powers to help them,' added a third.

'We were not without helpers ourselves,' said a fourth.

'If it had not been for the cowardice of *some*,' scowled a discontented fellow, shooting sidelong glances at some of his companions, 'we might be feasting in the jade palace by now.'

'If you are talking of those who ran, remember, evil Chang, that you were among them.'

'I was not the first to run,' countered Chang.

'Nor the first to fight, that I remember.'

With a snarl and a yell, Chang leapt across the flames and

flung himself on to the monkey who had spoken. In a moment all was confusion. The monkeys danced and yelled in their rage, biting and swinging, each on each, paying off old scores, remembering old feuds and fights. Round and round the fire they rolled, singeing their tails, screaming with the pain of

the firebrands on their feet, until the ground was a mass of struggling arms and legs. Only one stood apart, Wang, the smallest of them all, who watched their gambols with half a smile. Suddenly, his eyes gleaming, he swung with a long, blood-curdling scream on to the highest branch overhanging the clearing.

The rest, startled, and thinking some enemy was coming, stopped their fight in a moment, and gazed upwards. Having prepared the silence that he wanted, Wang spoke.

'Fine fools,' he yelled, shrilly. 'Fools and dunces, to waste your scratches on your friends, your bites on monkeys. Where are the Pekine-e-se?' he sneered. 'Save your teeth for the yellow gentlemen, the little lions, who feed on antelopes' milk.'

The monkeys scowled and chittered, prowling round the fire, licking their bites and scratches.

'Come down, O wise Wang,' said one, 'and let us make a

plan to revenge ourselves on the yellow people, with their palaces and pagodas.'

For these monkeys were jealous of the Pekinese.

So Wang swung nonchalantly down, with his right leg and his right arm – for on his left hand he had a bent and crooked thumb – and they gathered round the fire again, piling on more sticks.

'What can we do?' said the first monkey. 'We have tried a raid across the plains and a pitched battle.'

'We do not wish to try *that* again,' said another, rubbing his wounded leg.

'We must try a plot – we must work in secret and by stealth,' said someone.

Wang stroked his face and peered through his fingers, first one way and then the other.

'We must send a spy,' he said.

There was silence for a moment; only the fire sang as the sap burst from the green wood.

'But who will get entrance to the kingdom? We should be recognised at once, and sent to swing by our tails.'

'They would melt us for their medicine.'

'Cowards as well as fools,' thought Wang, but aloud he said, 'I will go to the Great Wall, and by my pranks I will be accepted. Meanwhile, you shall approach into the little hills behind the palace of the Emperor and hide in the forests there, outside the wall. But be careful to avoid the plains, for guards are posted all round the walls on look-outs. And do not approach the jade temple, near the northern wall, for there the five-toed Imperial dragons wait, watchful, pretending to be stone. But do not be deceived by that. They are as alive as a swinging ape, and more powerful. I shall set off tonight, taking the southerly road over our mountains. You shall collect such things as you will need for some time, and follow later, waiting cautiously till I give you some sign. And if I die, I die.'

They watched the silver figure of Wang

And Wang took nothing in his hands, but across his back slung a small pouch filled with acorns. Then he set off between the trees, swinging ahead of the rest, who followed more slowly, one after one, from branch to branch. Deep, deep into the forest they swung, for miles and miles, until gradually the trees grew thinner and the bushes less, and the scrub dwindled. They were coming out on to the other side. Suddenly they saw the figure of Wang silhouetted against the moon, swinging clear of the trees. Then they emerged themselves on to the slope and stood in a little band in the bare moonlight. The monkeys chattered, for the moon was full and they feared its brilliance. Backing into the forest, they watched the silver figure of Wang picking its way delicately between the rocks and bushes. When they could no longer tell Wang from the rock shadows, they turned sadly away into the trees and made for the forest depths once more.

3. The Juggler from Mandalay

Wang journeyed for three days and three nights. While he walked, or swung, or rested, he worked out plans in his cunning mind for entering the Pekinese kingdom. Once he passed a laurel bush with large leathery leaves, and picking some of these, he made himself a mask and put it carefully into his pouch.

On the second day he met a caravan of Mongols with mules and donkeys, making for the great far-off plains to the north of China. They had with them silk and spices, which they had bought in the markets of Chinese cities in exchange for wool. Wang amused them with tricks, and in return obtained a small cap of horsehair with a red silk tassel which he immediately began to wear, a pair of scarlet gloves and a lute. That night, when he had made his fire and eaten his supper beneath a clump of trees, he began to cut the most extraordinary capers. Putting on his cap, his mask and his gloves, he leapt from branch to branch of the trees, whooping and singing. He hung by his legs and played his lute, swinging gently backwards and forwards in time to the monkey song. Then he would hang by his feet, clasping his hands together. First gently, and then higher and higher he swung until he suddenly loosed his hold and flew through the air, landing safely on another tree. Wang continued these antics for some time, until all the stars came out in the velvet sky and rushed past him as he swung head downwards or somersaulted through the air. Finally he chose a safe, high branch above his fire, ate some more nuts and sat chuckling and hugging himself in the gloaming, watching the moon rise through the branches.

'Cuts and capers!' exclaimed the monkey. 'If only Wang

the Wise can get past those guards and show the Emperor and his ladies some of his tricks,' he said to himself, 'he will be on the way to finding out all he wants to know about the Pekinese.' And he slept above his fire; for no lonely monkey would care to sleep on the ground in a strange place without a guard to watch.

The next day he journeyed with a will, knowing that he must be near the end of his travels. He was climbing now up the small range of hills which lay to the north of the Pekinese wall. Wang went cautiously, in case there should be patrols of Pekinese warriors as far abroad as this: but he met no one, and towards the end of the day entered the shadow of wooded slopes.

On the morning of the third day he was up before sunrise, and ahead of him he could see the trees thinning out and the pearly-grey sky between them. A few minutes later he stood on the grey hillside, looking from the north, in time to see the sun rising golden and clear as honey on his left hand. And there beneath him, spread out in the valley, the morning mist cloaking some parts and revealing others so that it looked like a land of clouds, lay the country of the Pekinese, secure inside its great walls. The sunbeams struck across the plain, touching the tips of the highest pagodas and palaces and temples with their early gold. Immediately below him Wang could just see, through the mist, the Imperial palace, and near by the jade temple of the dragon.

The monkey waited until the sun was high in the sky and the mist was all folded up and put away, and he could see, if he watched hard, the busy Pekinese coming and going in their fields and city. Dropping down from the hills, he strode along to the west outside the wall for a mile or two, until he came round to the main gateway of the kingdom. Each side of it, on top of the wall, were the guards' pavilions, their verandas edged with rich jewels. The gate was open, for merchants were bringing in their wares to the Pekinese market and pedlars setting up their stalls for a day in the streets. The monkey walked boldly up to the gateway and peered inside. At once a fierce guard, with gold ruff and square jaw, stood in his way.

'What is the traveller's business?' he demanded. 'No monkey can pass these gates.'

'I am a wandering juggler-monkey from Mandalay,' said Wang. 'I have come many miles, hearing of the beauty of your kingdom and the richness of your princes, in case I might by some means see these marvels and find favour by my tricks in the Imperial palace.'

And Wang suddenly leapt into the air and swung from the edge of a veranda, and as quickly dropped back again and stood before the guard, clasping his hands together and bowing humbly. This antic and the speech before it had attracted the attention of several more guards, who stood round evidently uncertain what to do. Should they bite the foreign devil instantly according to the oldest traditions of their race?

Wang suddenly leapt into the air

Or should they send and tell the warriors, or even the Emperor himself?

'An order is an order,' said the first Pekinese, 'and my order was not to let any of the despicable race of the monkeys into the kingdom.'

Wang bore this insult as best he could.

'But,' said another guard, 'was not the war-lord thinking only of the tribes from the north-west who are now scattered by our warriors to the ends of the forests?' He had rather enjoyed Wang's trick, and thought him an amusing fellow.

'You must know,' said another to Wang, 'that our troops have not long returned from defeating these tribes. Our Emperor is in no mood to be entertained by the gambols of monkeys, whether from Mandalay or heaven itself.'

Wang took a step or two away, looking as sad as he was able; and taking a handful of nuts from his pocket, began to juggle, first slowly and then faster and faster, until the air in front of him seemed to be full of nuts. The Pekinese guards stood entranced in spite of themselves.

'He seems a good enough fellow,' said one.

'Let us give him a chance, at least,' said another.

'Keep him here while I send a toad to the palace to know the Emperor's will,' said the first guard. And he dispatched one of a group of toad messengers who had gathered at a peephole near the gate and were watching the marvellous monkey with gaping mouths. The toad grumbled a bit (for he wanted to see Wang's tricks), but soon hopped off on his important errand, his orange eyes glinting in the sunlight.

'May it please your Imperial Majesty,' began the Orange-eyed Teller of Tidings, when he had been ushered into the Emperor's presence, 'to listen to the tale of a humble toad, who has found shelter in the kingdom of the Pekinese, protection from the green dragon. . . .'

'Come on, come on,' said the Emperor, who had just had

an interview with his Minister of Riches and was feeling impatient, 'do not spend all day in kow-towing. What is the message?'

'There is a juggler-monkey from Mandalay in the Imperial gateway,' said the toad, 'who suspends nuts in the air, ten thousand at a time, and all moving. He seeks admittance to our kingdom for the entertainment of our princes.'

'A monkey?' said the Emperor angrily, 'who talks to me of MONKEYS! Let them bite him instantly and send him about his business!'

'But,' said the toad boldly (for he was aching to see more of Wang's tricks), 'this monkey wears a cap with a red tassel, and red gloves, and carries a lute. He is no fighter, but a wandering fellow, making his living by antics.'

'If he wore a cap with a coral button and had nails as long as my leg, he should not enter my kingdom,' shouted the Emperor. For in China, only the very grandest folk wear coral buttons on their caps, and only the rich can let their nails grow long.

So the disappointed messenger hopped a pace or two backward, kow-towing, and was about to leave the room when the old Official, Tu Fu, who stood near the Emperor, spoke.

'If one so lowly might say a word,' he remarked, bowing, 'I would remind your Imperial Excellence that preparations for the wedding of the Princess are afoot. If this animal can really suspend ten thousand nuts at a time in the air, an achievement unknown in the Pekinese kingdom, he would indeed enliven our merrymaking. There could be no harm in seeing him at least.'

'Have we enough cash to employ a monkey as a clown?' growled the Emperor to his Minister of Riches.

'We need not pay him much if we give him his food,' muttered the Minister in reply, twitching his whiskers nervously.

'We will see him,' said the Emperor to the toad.

And so the cunning and mischievous Wang was let into the kingdom. He delighted the Emperor and his court with his pranks, and even Stars in a Dark Pool, who was frightened at first, had to laugh when he danced a sugar plum on the end of his nose, or tossed a spray of peach blossom into her lap as he swung from the roof of the palace.

At first Wang was guarded closely by troops of Pekinese, who bit his heels if he walked a step out of the way, as he did often to look at the toymaker's stall in the street. (The monkey loved toys, singing-birds and musical boxes with silver handles, for he had never seen such things.)

He was locked into his pavilion at night, too, and let out only when the Emperor sent for him. All this Wang bore, hoping that soon his chance would come, that in time he would be permitted to move freely among the Pekinese. There was one thing he would never do: he refused utterly to remove his mask from his face or his gloves from his hands. The guards could not understand this, but being tolerant of the customs of other races, let him alone. And he behaved so well that soon they lessened their guard over him, sometimes allowing him to walk to the palace without handcuffs, and even to talk to the people he met on the way.

4. Plots and Poison

The artful Wang never forgot why he had come to the Pekinese kingdom, but kept his eyes and ears open to the comings and goings at the palace and the talk he heard around him. And much as he schemed, he seemed to be no nearer to the longed-for revenge upon the little yellow people. Should he try and poison the Emperor? He had no poison. Or blow up the Imperial palace? He had no gunpowder. Should he bribe one of the guards along the wall to let in his companions who would be waiting outside the city? He had very little cash. None of these plans seemed possible. Then one night, as it chanced, something happened which gave him an idea.

Wang was walking home after performing as usual at the Emperor's palace. He lived in a small house near the wall, next to the main gateway and close to the guards' houses, so that if he should misbehave there would be soldiers at hand to bite him. As he trotted along towards his pavilion, his Pekinese guards snuffling casually behind him, he noticed a light in the window of a house at a little distance from the road. He could see, too, a row of lanterns, pink and yellow and red and orange, strung between the trees before the house. This surprised Wang, for most of the Pekinese had gone to bed; and full of curiosity, he went up to see if there were anyone in the garden.

Once inside the gateway, he found himself walking along a little path between seas of blossom, dimly visible in the light of the lanterns, growing upon the daintiest, the tiniest, the prettiest trees he had ever seen. He was in the garden of a grower of dwarf trees, who soon approached him as he stood admiring a clump of flaming azaleas. The grower carried a lantern on a stick and a small can, and was evidently still busy watering his precious plants.

'I came up to see if there was any trouble,' said Wang, bowing politely, 'for yours is the only house with lights that I have passed tonight.'

The tree grower had heard of the monkey, and seeing the guards behind him, was quite disposed to be friendly. He showed Wang an almond tree, only eight inches high, and minute pear trees and plum trees all snowy with blossom, and prunus trees no bigger than Wang's legs, and peach trees curved and pretty with their pink flowers, and cherries hung with bundles of bloom, and stunted pines and firs growing in his rock garden where tiny waterfalls played.

'But why do you work so late?' said Wang, marvelling at the lovely scents around him.

'I am trying to get my best trees ready for the wedding feast,' said the gardener. 'And the old military Mandarin, whose son is marrying the Princess, has ordered as many trees as I can supply to decorate his gardens and halls and adorn the walls of the bridal chair.'

'And when is the wedding?' asked the monkey.

'Have you not heard?' said the gardener in surprise. 'Why, the whole world is talking of it. It is within a week from now; and the Princess, who is very fond of almond blossom, has ordered my best tree to make sprays for her hair.'

Wang had, of course, heard talk of the wedding, as the folk in the palace chattered about it at evening time when he was playing his pranks. But he had not heard how soon it was to be, nor had he thought much of it.

'Pagodas and palaces!' ejaculated the monkey, as a wicked notion entered his head. The Princess was to marry the son of a general, perhaps one of the very Pekinese warriors who had succeeded in routing his own tribe. What a revenge it would be to steal her away, and carry her off on the day before her wedding, perhaps to marry her himself! For Wang had often admired Stars in a Dark Pool, as she sat demurely in the palace hall.

'Pekinese and peaches!' he exclaimed softly as he turned away; but aloud he said good night to the tree grower, and walked home wrapped in thought. The gardener's words had reminded him of the Pekinese custom of marriage, how the bridegroom sent a special sedan chair the night before to fetch the bride to his house the next day. For in China, weddings take place not in the temple, but at the bridegroom's house.

'Now, if only,' thought the monkey, 'Wang the Wise can find out the bridegroom's house, and there discover the right chair, he could be carried to the palace with the greatest of ease, and the rest will follow. Stars and secrets!' And the mischievous monkey chuckled.

'What amuses you, O Wang?' said the guards.

'Only the tassel of my cap tickling my neck,' said he.

Wang knew that he must waste no time in learning all he could about the city and countryside. So from this moment, instead of practising his tricks in his spare time, he would ask his guards to go with him for long walks. All round and about Wang would lead them, behind the Emperor's palace, near the green jade temple, by the houses of wealthy mandarins and the fields of the rice growers and fruit farmers. And all the time he asked questions. The unsuspecting guards thought he was entranced with the beauty of their land and answered all he wished to know. Soon there was not much that Wang did not know. He knew each gate out of the kingdom, each bridge over a stream, each place on the wall where a sentry was posted. He knew where the bridegroom lived, and where the Princess and her maids would play. (But as soon as he had discovered the house of the military Mandarin, the great General Puffer, father of the amber-faced warrior, he was careful not to pass too close to it by daylight.)

And so the days crept by, the first day of the week, the second, the third. On the fourth day of the week, which happened also to be market day, Wang was strolling with his guards through the gaily coloured stalls, when he noticed the booth of an apothecary who sold herbs and medicines and spices, cinnamon, and scent from the flowers of the benzoin shrub, drugs made from the bark and wax-like buds of the magnolia, incense from the wood of the yew tree, and many another aromatic substance. All were neatly labelled, and set out in rows. Among them, Wang noticed some little packets tied with red string and labelled with green labels, marked 'POISON'.

'I am greatly troubled with rats in my house,' said the artful monkey, turning casually to one of his guards. 'I don't know if one or two of these packets would help to rid me of the vermin.'

The guards looked at the apothecary and then at Wang.

Wang buying poison

'I can assure you, nothing is better for rats than my poison,' said the chemist to the guards.

'Have you enough to pay for it?' asked they.

'Oh yes,' said the monkey, producing cash from his pouch. In return he received three little packets of poison. Wang chuckled as they walked away.

'What amuses you, O monkey?' said one of his guards.

'Only the thought of the innocent rats who will eat my poison,' said he, smiling a secret smile.

5. The Juggler Disappears

The amber-faced warrior himself, busy with the preparations for his wedding, had not yet seen the marvellous monkey performing his tricks at the Emperor's court. He had heard tales of his pranks, how he would somersault in the air above the Pekinese, and would spirit the singing-bird from its cage, making it perch upon the highest tip of the Imperial throne.

'By the gods of the palace,' muttered Amber Face, as he trotted along his father's verandas, seeing that all the bunches of hanging glass were tinkling a different note, in readiness for his wedding, 'I hope that the fellow will play no pranks with the Princess.'

The young Mandarin was, to tell the truth, a little bit jealous to think of any monkey performing before his Princess, whom he called 'Winkit' for love of her twinkling eyes.

'Nevertheless,' added he, stopping to pick a spray of waxy white camellias for the bridal chamber, 'I am too taken up with my own affairs just now to look after the Emperor's as well.' For he was full of eagerness and pride, and not a little conceited to think that he was to marry the Princess the next morning.

He turned to go into the house, but was stopped by the sound of bearers' feet, carrying a chair. It was Chu-i of the Red Coat, who had been among the guard at the Emperor's parade that afternoon, and had come to visit his friend with news of the palace.

'Welcome, O Chu,' said the warrior, kow-towing as Chu leapt from the chair.

'I hope all is ready?' said Chu, shaking his paws in greeting.

'All is finished, even, I believe, the food and wine,' said the warrior, beaming. 'And there on the veranda stands the bridal chair decorated with the Imperial dragons and the three curling fish of my family.'

'Let us sit in the cool of the evening,' said he, when Chu-i had admired the chair, 'and drink tea together.'

And as they sat sipping the fragrant potion, Chu-i told his friend of the Princess.

'She wore a gown stitched with peach blossom,' said Chu-i, 'and in her hair, the petals of the peach.'

The warrior sighed for pleasure as he sat in his bamboo chair.

'And did she look happy?' he asked.

'As happy as the Immortals in the gardens of the Queen of the West,' replied Chu. 'And when the monkey with the red-tasselled cap played on his melodious lute, I thought she would faint for joy!'

'By the seven gems!' exclaimed the Mandarin, 'I cannot understand why the Emperor should let in a monkey to our kingdom!' For he was jealous to hear of him. 'Tell me about him,' he added gruffly. 'What is he like? Can any number of juggler's tricks make up for the fact that monkeys are our enemies?'

'He is small and very nimble, and he wears only a cap, a mask and a pair of red gloves,' said Chu-i.

'Where does he come from?'

'From Mandalay, where he learnt, they say, his juggling tricks. He tosses twenty preserved peaches in the air, making patterns with them which are always changing. They say he will never take off his mask and his gloves, even in his own pavilion.'

'But why will he not take off his mask and his gloves?' said the warrior. And if he was uneasy before, he was more uneasy when he heard this. And the more Chu-i talked of the monkey, the more unhappy he became, until he suddenly

I cannot understand why the Emperor should let in a monkey

sprang to his feet yapping with anxiety.

'O, trusted friend, Chu,' he said, 'can you remember the smallest, the most agile, the cunningest of all the monkey horde? He who swung the furthest, he who had upon his left hand a bent and crooked thumb?'

Chu-i turned pale with terror.

'Can you not see,' continued the Mandarin, now thoroughly alarmed, 'why this fellow will not take off his gloves? The city and court swarm with the Imperial guards and soldiers who fought the monkeys, and who might recognise the wretch by his face or his thumb!'

'Supposing it should be him! What dreadful plots is he making against our kingdom?' said Chu-i, who had by this time recovered his wits.

'We must go to the palace at once,' said Amber Face. 'We must speak to the Official of the Court without delay.'

And the frightened Pekinese called for two sedan chairs of blue bamboo, and were borne off to the palace by eight running servants, with short tunics and black boots, their lanterns swinging as they ran.

No sooner were the bobbing lanterns out of sight, and the veranda quiet again, than a crouching, mysterious figure emerged from the thick clump of rhododendron and camellia bushes which lay to the side of the Mandarin's house.

'Plots and poisons!' whispered a voice. 'Only just in time did I escape!' and Wang chuckled softly, peered about him, and then rose to his feet.

'He! He! He! The foolish Pekinese,' he said, 'have even been kind enough to provide a chair for my journey! But first I will steal round to the kitchen, now that the cooks have left their sweets and bakemeats to cool, and I will poison the wine and food. Then if I fail to steal the Princess, some revenge at least will be certain!'

And he smiled as he crept towards the back of the house. But he had not gone far when he heard the patter of footsteps on the path, and the swish of Pekinese tails.

'Dragons and fishes,' muttered the monkey, dodging back to the veranda to hide there. The steps came nearer, and the lantern light approached, and Wang, as there was nowhere else to hide, hopped inside the chair until whoever it was should pass by. However, the steps did not pass him. They stopped at the chair, and four Pekinese bearers, grunting at the weight, lifted his hiding place on its poles and set off towards the city. Peering cautiously through the curtains, the monkey saw that they were making for the Emperor's palace.

'Only just in time again,' said he hugging himself with delight. 'Better to have caught the chair, than missed it poisoning the feast!' And he danced a tiny jig inside.

'Do not roll so,' said one of the back Pekinese snappily, to those in front.

'I never in all my life carried so heavy a chair,' said his partner. 'What is it made of? The tusks of elephants, instead of bamboo.' And he swore under his breath, his tongue rolling from his mouth as he trotted.

Meanwhile the two young warriors had already reached the palace.

'Let us in, let us in!' cried Amber Face, putting his lion-gold head out of the window when the chairs stopped. 'We must see the oldest Official on important business.'

Seeing who was in them, the guard let the chairs through, although by this time it was rather late.

'O, Tu Fu,' began the warrior, when the old man, fetched by a servant, came running from his bed to meet them.

'What is amiss that brings you into the palace so late?' queried the Official, flustered and flattered and wishing to be of service. And he hastily removed his nightcap and stuffed it up his sleeve.

'O wise Official,' said Amber Face, 'who is this monkey who juggles before the Emperor? What is his name, and where does he come from? And who let him in? We think he is one of our deadliest enemies. Send messengers quickly to fetch him to the palace and put an extra special guard on him. Or let us go ourselves!'

And the Pekinese explained about the red gloves and the crooked-thumbed monkey, speaking very fast and both together.

'Gently, gently, one at a time,' protested the old Official, 'I can make out nothing while you both yap, and you will wake the Emperor who sleeps close by.'

It was very dark under the juniper trees, and in the stillness a nightingale poured out its liquid song. No moon shone in the sky, and Amber Face and Chu-i could just see the puzzled, wrinkled face of the old Pekinese in the light of the lanterns.

'Send at once,' pleaded Chu, 'and we will explain afterwards. All may be well; but if any plot is afoot, we must stop it first and talk later.'

So the old Official awoke more guards and sent them bobbing off to the monkey's house near the wall. Then, stepping into another chair and bidding the two Pekinese follow, he set off after the guards.

Soon after they had gone, the guard at the gate was aroused once more by the sound of footsteps. This time it was the bridal chair.

'Let us through!' called the Pekinese dumping their burden and mopping their brows. 'The Princess's chair, sent from the Mandarin's house!'

Once more the growling guard unlocked the gate, and across the Imperial gardens went the little procession to the Princess's quarters. When they reached the passage outside her door, the bearers put down the chair with a sigh and received a handsome cumshaw (or tip) from Golden Bells, and a collection of sweetmeats and tit-bits from the maidens in the hall who gathered round to praise the beauties of the chair. One even peeped through the curtains, but the artful Wang had taken the precaution of hiding under the seat.

'And when you come in the morning,' said Golden Bells, giving them their last instructions, 'you will know by the spray of almond blossom hung upon the screen in the hall that the Princess is ready. Then pick up the chair and bear it to the wedding.'

And the bearers trotted off, sucking their comfits, while all the Princess's maidens clapped their little white paws.

As Amber Face, Chu-i and the Official of the court approached the monkey's house, they saw that there was a light burning in one of his windows.

'He is practising his tricks,' said Chu-i.

'We will teach him a trick or two,' said his friend.

And tumbling over each other in their eagerness to get into the door as the guards unlocked it, the three entered the house.

But the monkey was nowhere to be seen.

6. Lantern Light and
a Lost Princess

The Pekinese gazed at each other in the blankest dismay,
unable to believe their eyes.

'Come,' said the Official, 'unlock the inner door. Doubtless
the monkey has gone to bed and forgotten to put out the
light.'

So the guards unlocked the second door which led into
Wang's small bedroom. This was in pitchy-darkness, but
through the gloom they could hear grunts and snuffles and
the turning and tossing of a restless sleeper.

'The monkey sleeps uneasily,' Chu muttered, as he fetched
the lamp.

But when they peered into the room, they found no Wang
on the bed, but his two unhappy guards tied up and muffled,
tossing from side to side in their efforts to escape. The amber-
faced warrior groaned and whined with anxiety.

'Raise the guards,' he ordered, 'and tell them to wake the
soldiers. The monkey is at large in our kingdom, and we must
search high and low until we find him. You, my faithful
friend,' said Amber Face turning to Chu, 'shall run to the
Princess's quarters in the Emperor's palace and make sure
that all is well there. I shall lead the soldiers on their search.
You, O esteemed and worthy Official,' said he to the old man,
who was rubbing his paws and rolling his eyes with fright,
'wait and hear the story of these unfortunate guards.'

And the warriors ran off, waving their standards of pomp,
and yapping with rage and terror.

And soon the streets of the city and the fields outside it
were alight with rows of bobbing lanterns, and noisy with

excited war shouts, as the Pekinese guards made their search.
Up and down the streets they went, through the dim and
gloomy forests, where shafts of lantern light, searching the
branches of the trees, awoke the sleeping birds; over the

bridges they swayed, shining their lanterns into the black
mysterious water where the lotus floated. The guards along
the wall were questioned, each in turn, and warned to let no
one through. The green dragons at the river gates, who
guarded the wall where the rivers flowed out of the kingdom
into the country beyond, were told to be extra watchful, to
keep, in fact, two eyes open instead of only one. (For most
clever dragons can sleep with one eye and watch with the
other.)

The Pekinese population, awoken by the clatter, came running to its doors and was told to search the courtyards and
barns for the mischievous intruder. Even the temple was
searched and the courtyard where the maidenhair trees grew
and the house of the bonzes, who were busy burning joss
sticks in the dark of the night.

The young Mandarin, his amber jaw set in determination
and his ruff standing up straight with anger led the search

round his father's house, the house of the great General Puffer who, awoken from his bed, came shuffling with the rest, and even went himself to the palace of General Snorter, his elderly friend, to beg his help.

Meanwhile, the red-coated Chu-i went to the palace of the Emperor and inquired of the guards there.

'Only the bearers from the military Mandarin's house, bringing the bridal chair, have entered the gates since nightfall,' said the guard. 'And they arrived just after you and the worthy amber-faced warrior.' And he grunted priggishly through his whiskers.

'But is there any way else a monkey might enter?' said the anxious Chu-i.

'It would hardly be possible that he should escape all the guards,' said he, 'but perhaps you should search the grounds and palace to satisfy yourself. The Princess's quarters are at the furthest edge of the pavilion.'

So Chu-i and his faithful band trotted off towards the palace.

The wicked Wang, who had been watching the search from a window since the Pekinese ladies went to bed, and chuckling to think of his enemies looking for him in vain, was horrified to see the lanterns approaching the Princess's hall.

'O fool that I am to rejoice too soon,' said he. And he sprang back into the chair and hid trembling under the seat.

Chu-i came to the hall, knocked at the door, and sent messages to Golden Bells.

'Is the Princess safely in her bed?' he asked the maiden.

'Safe and sound, and already asleep,' replied she.

'Do not wake and alarm her, then,' said Chu, 'but let us search this part of the palace to make sure all is well.'

Golden Bells unlocked the door and the red-coated warrior searched, all round and about, behind the screens, under the chairs, in the cupboards, through all the Princess's rooms.

But nobody thought to look in the chair.

Finally, satisfied at last, the warrior bade the maidens good night, and marched away from the Imperial palace towards the market place. Here after some time gathered the rest, disappointed also in their search.

'There is no doubt,' said the excellent Generals, both yawning into their wide sleeves, 'that this fellow, wishing for some

reason to leave our kingdom, has leapt the wall where the pine trees grow and made off before the hunt began. But see that extra guards are posted in case he still lurks in the land.'

And they trotted off to their beds, muttering and snuffling. But Amber Face and his friend, less easily satisfied, stayed looking and talking till it was long past the middle of the night. Then they too gave up the search and went to bed.

Wang, crouching under the seat of the chair, waited until it was quiet again. After what seemed many hours to the impatient monkey, he stole out of the hall and into the chamber where the Princess lay, her maid curled up at her feet.

'Toads and wizards!' said the monkey softly. 'I can hardly carry two. But if I leave one tied up, they will see her in the morning and, anyway, she is pretty enough, and will do to wait upon us.'

So he tied up Golden Bells first, muffling her with a silken sash, and the Princess after. The gallant Pekinese tried to bite and yap, but Wang was stronger than they, and he put them both in a silken pillow case and slung them over his shoulder. Then he crept to the window (not forgetting to hang the spray of almond blossom on the screen) and let himself down on to the north side of the pavilion.

Stalking along by the wall of the house within the veranda, Wang nearly fell over a sleeping figure. Around him stood little pots of almond trees, glimmering in the wavering light before dawn. It was the tree grower, who, in his eagerness to cut his blossoms and weave them freshly for the Princess, had brought them up the night before and was sleeping in the courtyard. Over him lay his long cloak, and near by his shallow straw hat.

'Toads and wizards,' said the monkey again, 'I am lucky!' And he tied up the poor gardener in his own tunic, stole both hat and cloak, and picking up the gardener's yoke, on each end of which was a round basket, he crept steathily on. When he thought it safe to stop, he dressed up in the cloak and hat, and put a Pekinese in each basket, tying them down with the pillow case. Then he made boldly for the wall.

'I am certainly the cleverest of monkeys,' he said to himself. 'But I will not speak to soon.'

'Who is it approaches so close to the temple of the green dragon, and at dead of night?' said the guard on the wall.

'I am a tree grower,' said Wang, 'and I am going up to the forested slopes before dawn to cut fresh branches for the Emperor's halls.'

'I have orders to let no one out,' said the sleepy guard,

'while that monkey is still free. But I suppose you know your own business.'

And he unlocked the gate.

Wang walked sedately out, hardly daring to believe his good fortune. His face was well hidden by the wide straw hat and he took care that the long sleeves of the cloak should cover his black shiny hands as he passed the guard. But if he could have seen the temple at that moment, he would have noticed that one of the stone dragons winked its eye. He walked steadily up the lower slopes, cursing softly at the weight of his bundles and picking his way with difficulty between bushes and rocks, in the half light. When he was in the shelter of the trees, he began to skip and jump a little (rather clumsily, for the two Pekinese were heavy on his shoulders), and chuckle to himself, so elated did he feel at his easy escape. He waited until he was deep within the forest, and then let out his cautious monkey call to summon his friends. At first there was no reply, only a shivering in the tops of the branches. Wang called again.

'Come, O monkeys. It is I, Wang, escaped from the kingdom of the Pekinese !'

He listened. And he heard rustle after rustle, creak after creak, as his friends gathered through the trees, peering to see if it were really Wang, and then swinging towards him with excited low calls. Waiting only to unbind the Pekinese ladies, who sat with staring eyes, shivering with fright in their little baskets, the band set off for the mountains, yelping and chittering. When they were further away and it was safe to stop, they would make, they decided, a covered chair of bamboo and creepers for the ladies to ride in.

Meanwhile, day dawned in the land of the Pekinese, and at the appointed time the four chair-bearers came briskly up to the Princess's quarters. Seeing the spray of almond on the ebony screen, they proceeded along the passage, picked up the bridal chair and bore it away, while all the Princess's little

maidens stood in two rows in the gardens, bowing, to watch it go. Through the streets they trotted, where crowds of happy Pekinese threw petals and yapped with pleasure. The

benign Emperor, watching from his highest verandas, lifted his paws in blessing, and the kind Empress wept a few tears on to the fluffy shoulder of her favourite maid.

As the chair stopped in front of the dwelling of General Puffer, his son, the amber-faced warrior, modest but magnificent in his mandarin's robes, stepped down himself to open the door. His heart beat and his eyes filled with pleasure, while every hair on his amber face quivered with excitement for thinking of the bright eyes and sooty face of his little bride. But when he opened the door and peered lovingly inside, no twinkling eyes met his, no paw was stretched out in welcome. Horrified, Amber Face looked again, and saw only the monkey's cap and red gloves neatly folded on the seat.

7. The Beginning of the Journey

Hardly waiting to tell his father and mother, who were seated at that moment in the hall ready to receive their son and daughter, the distracted Mandarin set off in his own chair for the palace, his faithful friend Chu-i following behind.

'The Princess, the Princess!' panted poor Amber Face when he reached the palace. 'Where is the Princess?'

'She has but half an hour ago left the palace,' said the puzzled guard, 'borne in her chair.'

'The chair was empty, O watchful ones. The Princess must still be here.' And he ran on into the hall.

'What,' said the genial Emperor in surprise, as he saw the warrior bowing before him, 'can the wedding be over so soon?'

'The Princess is lost,' sobbed the young Mandarin. 'And only the cap and gloves of the wicked monkey were in the chair!'

At this moment a servant came running from the Princess's quarters.

'Golden Bells, the Princess's maiden, has disappeared,' he gasped, 'and we do not know where to look for her. And the tree grower, who was sleeping in the courtyard, has been found bound and muffled!'

'Alas!' said the Emperor, 'there has been some mischief here.'

And in the greatest alarm he listened to the tale of the missing monkey. The tree grower, who was revived with a little hot peach tea, was unable to tell much, except that a figure like that of the monkey had bound him before he was properly awake and had gone off with his cloak and baskets.

'We will question the guard near the temple gate,' said Amber Face, 'for it sounds as if he went that way.'

The poor guard confessed that he had let a tree grower through very early that morning before it was light.

'O careless Pekinese,' said the Emperor, 'you deserve a worse punishment, but I shall only imprison you for a month, and feed you on black bread and water. Take him away.'

And the guards led him off, his standard of pomp dragging between his legs.

'We must set out at once to find them,' said the warriors. 'Perhaps they will not have gone very far. And if we cross the plain instead of going round by the wooded hills we shall be quicker than they.'

So Amber Face and Chu-i picked out ten of their most trusted soldiers and told them to be ready in less time than a heron takes to swallow a frog. And while Chu had them assembled in the market place, and drilled them, the two old Generals came up with armour and spears, and fussed round, getting them ready.

'Indeed, my son,' said General Puffer to the Prince who was nearly a Prince, 'would it not be wiser to take more than ten warriors? Why not get ready half the army to go after

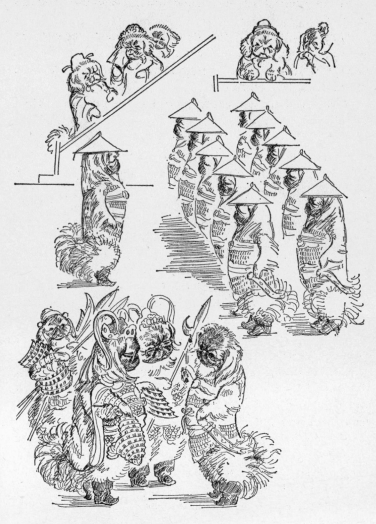

Chu had them assembled in the market place and drilled them

these villains?'

'We shall have to swim rivers and climb rocks, push through forests and feed on what we find. And it is easier to feed a dozen than a thousand,' replied Amber Face.

So they took very little with them beside their light armour: each carried a small pack with enough food and drink for a few days, and some carried a charm to keep them from

evil. And the Emperor brought Amber Face a carved jade dragon and bade him keep it safely all the way; whereas his father gave him a tiny bottle made of a single chryosprase, with the three fish carved round it, and containing some shredded rhinoceros horn in case of sickness. Amber Face and Chu-i took also some small presents in their pouches, in case they had need of them to obtain help on the way.

Then, while Chu-i took the band to the Mandarin's house to feed well on the forgotten wedding feast, sharks' fins, and the breasts of quails and sweet fruits and nuts, the amber warrior hurried to the temple. Here he prayed to the champion of warriors, Kuan-ti, who helps his people against harmful animals, and all enemies. As the Pekinese left the temple after burning his incense sticks, he passed close by the stone dragons, relations of those who guard the Pekinese kingdom.

The one on his right winked his eye to the warrior and whispered in his ear, 'Keep always northward, and do not fear, for the Princess and her maiden live still. But when the jade dragon turns pale, then hasten, for the Princess's life is waning.'

The warrior thanked the dragon courteously, and went to join his men.

And so the valiant Pekinese were ready to leave the kingdom, scarcely an hour after the discovery. Through the streets from the market place they went, while the Emperor's own guards played hand drums, and the bamboo pipers piped a sorrowful march. The city, only an hour ago so happy, was now thronging with sad and long-faced Pekinese who watched them go with anxious whines and sniffs. The two Generals and the Emperor himself, with a host of other Pekinese, watched from the walls as the warriors left the kingdom, jostling shoulder to shoulder, ears blown back and tails up. Soon they were only an amber ripple on the surface of the

distant plain. Then the Pekinese went sadly home, half afraid that they would see none of the gallant band again.

But Amber Face and Chu and their soldiers trotted on with hope in their hearts, singing songs to keep up their courage. And Chu-i, who was a little of a poet, made up a song for them to sing.

BATTLE SONG OF THE PEKINESE

Trot and jostle
Jostle and sway,
On we go
The Pekinese way.

Who has felt
Our warriors bite
Never risks
A second fight

Even Wang
The monkey king
Far prefers
His monkey ring,

May the valiant
Kuan-ti
Plague the monkeys
As they fly.

Not a falter
Of fear we feel,
Battle ruff up
And lifted tail.

Who has heard
Our army growl
Sets his best leg
For his hole.

When the fearful
Pekinese
Chase him to
His forest trees.

May the great
Jade Emperor
Bring us safely
Home once more.

When they had sung this song more than many times, they found that they were approaching the wide river which skirts the western side of the plain wherein their kingdom stands, and runs down from the mountains far to the north. They had travelled many miles across the plain and daylight was beginning to waver. Ahead of them the great golden sun was dropping sleepily down behind the furthest mountains, and the bright and beautiful sunset clouds, red, and gold and pea-cock blue, settled down over him like a coverlet. Soon the sky was a pearly grey and getting always darker.

'Tonight, we will camp on the banks of this river,' said Amber Face, 'for it will soon be too dark to see our way.'

So the Pekinese laid down their packs and busied them-selves with collecting sticks and dry grass for their fire.

Choosing a small green bay, sheltered by bushes and boulders from the windy plain, they made their camp and cooked their food, and were soon asleep and snoring, while two in turn kept watch under the stars.

Very early in the morning Amber Face and Chu-i were awake and discussing the way they should go.

'How much easier it would be, O Chu, if we had boats to follow this river to where it leaves the mountains.'

'We might build rafts,' said Chu doubtfully, 'and row them along with poles.'

'Or we might weave a sail of fine grass,' added Amber Face.

'That would take longer than walking by the river bank,' said his friend smiling.

But at this moment there came sliding round the bend of the river a fishing junk, its red sails set. It was occupied only by a thoughtful cormorant, who was evidently watching for fish.

When he came almost opposite the Pekinese encampment, he lowered his sails, cast his anchor and sat quietly on the bows of his boat, his eyes bent on the water, and his fishing-line fixed beside him. As soon as he saw a fish tug the line, he would dive and bring it up in his beak. When he had done this several times and seemed satisfied with his haul, he sat solemnly watching the Pekinese; and Chu and Amber Face sat solemnly watching him in return. Then Amber Face spoke.

'Will you, O cormorant, expert in the catching of fish, carry us and our warriors up the river in your boat? For we are in a hurry to overtake some monkeys who have stolen away our Princess.'

The cormorant considered this in silence. Then he said —

'If you, O Pekinese warriors, will give me some strands of your esteemed tail fans to make new lines for my rods, I will carry you as far as I can go.'

And he brought his boat across.

So the delighted Pekinese, with all their bundles, boarded the junk, helped set the sails, and were soon sliding swiftly through the water.

8. Turtles and Fishes

Up the river they went, until the little bay which had been their home for one night was left far behind, and the mountains began to look nearer and darker. Then, too, they noticed that the river was getting narrower, and the bushes and rocks along its edge thicker. At last, when they had sailed for several hours, and had eaten a meal of broiled fish, cooked over the cormorant's stove, their silent companion turned to Amber Face and said —

'I am afraid I can carry you no further, for the river will soon become too shallow, and its banks too narrow for my boat.'

So the Pekinese, after pulling out some of their very best and longest tail hairs for him, picked up their bundles, thanked the kindly cormorant with many bows, and stepped ashore on the rocky bank. Then the cormorant brought his boat around, lowered the sails, waved to the warriors and drifted gently downstream with the current.

The Pekinese shook and stretched themselves, pleased to feel the dry land under their feet once more, and set their faces to the north, following the narrow path by the edge of the river. They talked little, for the path soon became uneven with boulders, and they were forced to walk in single file. When they had breath, they sang their battle song, and when they had not they clambered on thinking their own thoughts. Some thought of their friends in their far-off kingdom, some thought of what they would eat and drink when they got back, some, the more gloomy, wondered about the dangers to come. But Amber Face, walking ahead, thought of Stars in a Dark Pool and her black, silky face and bright eyes. And

Up the river they went

it occurred to him that he had not lately looked at his jade dragon to see if the Princess were alive and well. So he put his hand into his pouch to find it. By an evil chance, as he took his eyes off the path, he stumbled over a rock and fell,

and the little jade dragon rolled out of his paw and was lost in the depths of the river.

'O, Chu-i,' wailed the poor warrior, as the rest of the band came hurrying up from behind, 'I have lost the jade dragon which the Emperor bade me cherish safely against all danger!'

'Where has it fallen, O Amber Face?' said Chu. 'Perhaps we can by some means rescue it.'

And the warriors stood in a row on their fours along the bank, peering anxiously into the river. A waterfall came tumbling over a rocky shelf a little distance above them, and emptied itself into a deep dark pool with bubble and swirl and eddy. From the pool the water flowed steeply over another shelf, as if tipped evenly from a great basin. It was into the deep pool that the dragon had fallen.

'If we look all day and all night,' said Chu sadly, 'we shall see nothing in this pool. Had we not better go on after the monkeys?'

'I do not dare lose the jade dragon,' said poor Amber Face. 'Besides, how am I to tell whether the Princess lives or no, without it? Do you take the rest on, faithful Chu, and make a camp in the hills, for the day is drawing in. I will dive for my dragon into the depths of the pool.'

'You will be swept over the edge of the rapids,' said Chu, in fear, 'or dashed to pieces beneath the waterfall!' And he

begged his friend to stay on the shore. But Chu's entreaties were in vain.

'If I do not appear by nightfall,' said Amber Face, 'then come back and look for me. But now go on, and leave me to venture alone.'

So Chu went sadly on, leading the rest.

When they were out of sight the Pekinese took off his doublet and boots, laid them on the bank and stood on the edge staring into the water. Then he took a deep breath and dived. How cold it was, and how the water drummed in his ears! How very dark it was, too, down here! How would he ever see his green dragon, even supposing it had not been swept over the shelf? He reached the rocky bottom of the river, and with a great effort, opened his eyes, searching frantically among the sand and weeds for the dragon. The current was very strong, and the warrior found himself being swept into the middle of the river bed and carried downstream. With a last despairing look around him he came struggling to the surface, coughing and spluttering, and swam for the nearest land he could see. He scrambled up the bank on to a large, smooth stone, where he sat gasping for breath and shaking his whiskers.

'By the god of the river,' said he, when he could see out of his eyes again, 'I think I have landed on the other side of the stream! O dear, O dear,' he said, looking about him. 'Another minute and I should have been over the edge of that torrent.' And he shivered with fright, standing up to shake the water from his coat.

'What's this? Hail stones and rain? I must go back home then,' croaked an old and sleepy voice from beneath him. Amber Face jumped with surprise as the stone he was standing on began to move. It was an old turtle.

'It's not rain, it's me!' he said, balancing with difficulty on the turtle's shell.

The old turtle stopped, craned his head round, blinked sleepily at him and said —

'Hey! What! Who are you, sitting on my house and dripping water down my neck? Speak up, my ears are not as good as they were!' He sounded so grumpy and graceless, that the warrior slipped quickly to the ground, and went round to his head end, kow-towing before him.

'I beg your pardon,' he began, 'I thought you were a stone —'

'What?' said the turtle again. 'I cannot hear you. Come a bit closer,' he croaked.

And the warrior made a trumpet of his wet paws and shouted into the turtle's ear.

'I said I was sorry, I mistook you for a stone, excellent turtle!'

The turtle thought for a moment and then said —

'Possibly because I am stone deaf. He! he! he!' And he laughed an old quavering laugh.

Amber Face laughed too, glad that he had not offended the turtle for good, and comforted to find a friendly person to talk to in his distress.

'Why are you so wet?' the turtle asked next. 'You are dripping water in my ear! Has it been raining?'

'No,' replied the warrior. 'But I have just dived into the river to rescue a dragon,' he explained, shouting as much of his story as he could into the turtle's ear.

'What do you say? You are a Pekinese Mandarin?' quavered the turtle. 'Why, let me see,' he said, 'I know your Emperor well. I used to live in his lotus pool when I was a boy. His name is Ti-Li, is it not?'

Amber Face stared, wondering, at the aged turtle.

'Oh, no,' he said, in surprise, 'the Emperor Ti-Li has been dead one hundred and twenty years, though of course I have heard tell of him. Our present ruler is the worthy and excellent Yen-Li, his great-great-great-great-grandson!'

'Well, well,' replied the turtle, 'you do not live for long in your kingdom, if that is the case.'

'If your aged-ness would excuse the question,' said the warrior, with esteem, 'how old are you?'

'Let me see,' muttered the turtle, 'I *think* I shall be one hundred and twenty-nine next birthday. Or maybe it is one hundred and thirty. I can never be quite sure. But that's nothing,' he continued in a tone full of memories, 'why, my eldest brother is nearly one hundred and fifty. And there are those in my pool,' and he waved his paw, 'who have lost count – altogether. I can remember the days when the Mongol monkeys invaded your kingdom. That is why our family moved, as far as I remember . . . We did not care for them. A sudden and savage race, they were . . . And now you have trouble with the monkeys again, eh?'

'Yes, indeed,' said Amber Face, coming back with a start from the mysterious past ages whence the turtle's words had carried him. 'I am on my way to rescue the Pekinese Princess, but I am held up for this dragon I have lost.'

'Perhaps I could find it for you,' quavered the turtle. 'My eyes are not so good now, but I can at least stay under the water as long as I choose. And I know the king who rules this river. A friendly carp he is, though young to be king. He's only seventy . . . where did you drop this precious dragon?'

'Over on the other side, and near that big ring of boulders on the bank,' said the warrior.

'Wait here,' said the turtle. 'I may be some time,' he said, 'for my race is slow but sure.'

And he slid into the river and was soon lost from sight. This was what Amber Face had hoped for, and he sat contentedly

on the bank, as the night fell, waiting for the turtle. Soon it
grew so dark that he could not see the other bank. He was
rather cold, too, because of his wet fur and the cheerless wind
which was blowing from behind him. So he jumped up and
trotted to and fro in the darkness.

Meanwhile the old turtle had reached the bottom of the
pool and had made his way to the far bank where he began
hunting carefully through the green forests of weeds and in
the little rocky bays of golden sand. He was busily shuffling
his way along when a large sentinel fish came swimming up,
opening and closing his mouth and looking surprised and
aggrieved.

'Speak up, my boy,' said the turtle chuckling, for the fish
looked very funny, opening and closing his mouth. 'I'm a
little deaf.'

But the fish, who had not spoken at all, looked even more
surprised and said : 'The king has sent me to find out what
you are doing in our kingdom.'

'Fiddle-de-dee,' said the turtle, 'I know your king well. Go
and tell the golden carp that it is his friend the turtle. On
second thoughts, I'll come myself,' he said.

So the fish turned and swam away down a long path of
golden sand, the turtle following as fast as he could behind
him. Inside the king's cave there was a huge commotion. Fish
of all kinds, large and small, spotted and scaled, striped and
ringed, were swimming with great concern round a young
fish, smaller than the rest, who was rolling and writhing,
twisting and turning in the strangest fashion.

'He has swallowed a small, hard dragon which fell into our
pool,' explained the king, when he had greeted the turtle.

'Exactly what I am looking for !' replied the delighted
turtle. 'Seize him by his tail and shake him,' he said to a large
fish near by.

So the young fish was shaken by his tail, long and hard :
and out at last came the green dragon and floated on to the

golden sand before the turtle's nose.

'This is, without doubt, the warrior's dragon,' he said, picking it up and tucking it under his shell, 'and I am much obliged to you for taking care of it.' And he patted the little fish on the head. 'And now, if you will excuse me,' he said, bowing to the king, 'I will be off.'

'There are river weeds, lotus buds, frog spawn and tender worms for dinner,' said the king, 'if you would care to stay.'

The turtle's mouth watered, but he thought of Amber Face waiting anxiously on the bank, and declined the invitation.

Up through the water he came, the dragon safely in his pocket, and landed close by the waiting warrior. Amber Face wagged his tail with joy as he saw his friend again and received the green dragon into his own paw. Then he mounted the turtle's back and was carried safely over the river.

'Farewell, O kind turtle,' said he, bowing low, 'and if ever I can do you a service, be sure that I will.'

'Farewell, brave Mandarin,' croaked the turtle. 'A few lotus buds from the Emperor's pool would not come amiss,' he added, swimming off into the darkness.

Amber Face looked about him, but at first could see nothing. Above him stretched the sky like a blanket, only a few lonely stars piercing its darkness. Then the warrior, groping his way along the bank, espied at a little distance a pile of clothes which were his, and on top of them, as if staring sadly into the river, he could discern the lonely form of the faithful Chu. Amber Face could hear him whining softly to himself with anxiety.

'Here I am, Chu-i! Here I am,' he called, scrambling along the path.

And Chu, leaping to his feet with a yap of joy, licked his friend's face many times and helped to dress him in his doublet and boots. Then they set off together for the camp, running and jumping to keep themselves warm, and pleased when they saw the bright fire at last and their fellows gathered round it.

9. Rain, Riddles and Rocks

That night, when the Pekinese were curled close together in a cave in the hillside, they heard the rain begin. Gently at first it fell and then more and more loudly until the air was full of its beating on the hillside. Their night's fire was soon scattered, and the guard at the door came inside and shook himself and swore softly. Looking out of the cave he saw in the dawn light that their path had become a young rivulet sweeping along pebbles and straws as it hurtled its way gurgling and gulping into the valley. That morning the sun rose pink and watery behind the grey clouds which masked the highest mountain peaks. It still rained when they were ready to set forth on their journey.

'Which path shall we take?' said Chu, anxiously. 'If we go on in this rain and mist we may come to grief, but we have no time to lose dallying here.'

'We will go up this path, hoping that the day will clear, and we shall be able to see the easiest pass across the mountains. This is a well-used track, and must lead somewhere,' replied Amber Face.

'I cannot see,' said one of the Pekinese, 'however we are going to cross the highest mountains at all.'

'We are not a climbing race,' said another, 'we have no hoofs and our legs are somewhat short.'

'We will meet that difficulty when we come to it,' said their wise leader; and with their heads bent against the weather they went on up the hillside. And still it rained, until their standards of pomp were bedraggled, their paws muddied and the fur on their ears dripped water drops down their necks. Chu, who was leading them on, tried to sing, but the

Their heads bent against the weather

wind blew his weak voice mockingly away before it reached him who walked behind. A bit further on, he stopped and looked about him. Far below them they knew was the river in its valley; they could see nothing for the mist that shrouded it, but they heard its distant, swollen roar. Above them, wrapped in mystery, loomed the high peaks. At this moment the torrents became heavier, and Amber Face, afraid that the warriors might be swept from the path, led them aside towards an island of rocks to seek shelter.

'There is a cave in these rocks,' said Chu, eagerly.

'Let us get in, for the love of Heaven,' said the wet warriors, longing for warmth and shelter. And they all trooped into the dark mouth of a rocky opening.

'Not so fast, not so fast,' said a Voice from inside. 'Who are you to come tumbling into my home, disturbing my spells and meditations?'

'We seek only shelter from the storm,' replied Amber Face to the Voice.

'What brings you out on the mountain-side in such weather as this?' asked the hidden occupant of the cave.

'We are going on a journey, and can stop for nothing,' said Chu-i.

'You have interrupted me in my search for the stone of immortality. But, nevertheless, come in and be silent, until the rain has ceased to roar.'

And with these words there came forward from the depths of the cave the old Taoist hermit who lived there. He was dressed in a long robe made of many different pieces sewn together, round which he wore a double girdle. On his feet were sandals of straw, and he wore a kind of crown on his head. He carried a lantern in his hand, by the light of which he conducted the warriors further into his dwelling. There was a brazier of burning charcoal, warm and red, round which the cold and weary Pekinese were glad to huddle. On the floor there were other smaller braziers from which rose

up sweet-smelling vapours. Little jars of molten metal,
ladles of liquid gold, lay about the floor of the cave where
the wizard was working. But the Pekinese cared more for the
fire than these things.

'And whither is this journey,' said the old man, offering
them cakes baked of chestnut flour, 'which drives you on

even in the teeth of the wind and rain?' And he rubbed his
hands and shuffled his feet.

So the Pekinese explained all about their Princess and their
journey, and how they were making for the monkey forest
beyond the mountains.

'And can you tell us, O wise one, which way we should go
to cross the mountains? Where is the safest pass and how far
off?' ended Amber Face.

The wizard twirled his whiskers and was thoughtful as he looked at the little band gathered round his fire.

'There is no road over the mountains which a Pekinese can safely tread,' he answered. 'All the passes are bitter with rocks and snow or floating with slow rivers of ice.'

'How then shall we go?' said Chu-i.

'You can only travel and try,' said the wizard, and he went to his brazier and began chanting solemnly, half to himself and half to the warriors —

> *Those with beards, like any man,*
> *Climb and jump where no man can.*
> *Enemies to Pekinese*
> *You with sorcery may please.'*

'But what is the sorcery we are to say?' said Chu when the old man had finished.

The wizard looked at Chu and then went on slowly —

> *By the sword of Kuan-ti,*
> *By the Monarch of the Sky,*
> *By the Lady of the West,*
> *And the garden of the blest,*
> *Carry us beyond the snows*
> *Where the monkey forest blows.'*

'And who are we to say it to?' asked Amber Face, a little crossly. For the riddle seemed to him very difficult.

> *Say it when you see them come,*
> *But beware the hoof and horn,'*

replied the wizard. And no more would he say. So the puzzled Pekinese remembered all his words, resolving to unravel the riddle together as they went.

Going to the door of the cave, Chu discovered that the rain had stopped, and the clouds were splitting. So they bade the old muttering man goodbye and started off once more.

It was hopeful to see the sunlight shafting through the tattered clouds and clearing the misty mountains. And Chu did a little jump into the air, and all the rest followed him, for their coats were dry again and their toes warm, and even the thought of the snowy and rocky mountains could not dismay them.

As they marched merrily along they said the wizard's riddle over and over again, but the more they pondered, the less easy it became.

In a little while, their eyes upon the rocky peaks, they espied a tribe of shaggy goats picking their way delicately in a long line over a ridge above them.

'They are coming down towards us, those creatures,' said Amber Face, 'and I do not like the look of their horns.'

'Let us hide behind these rocks,' suggested one of the band.

'It is too late, they have seen us!' said another.

And it was true enough. The goats had begun to race madly down the slope towards them. The frightened Pekinese, taken by surprise, were scattering in all directions, when suddenly Chu said loudly —

' "But beware the hoof and horn!" Quick, the wizard's spell. Say it loudly, O Pekinese; do not be afraid of the mountain goats, who shall carry us over the rocks. Say it into their beards.'

So the Pekinese stood where they had run and chanted the verse all together. At once the leaping goats slowed their steps, and came fawning and ambling down the slope, with friendly eyes, to stand in a ring round the Pekinese.

'We are travellers for the land of the monkeys,' said Amber Face, 'but we cannot cross these peaks unless you help us.'

'Willingly we will help you,' said the obliging goats.

'Clamber upon our backs, holding tight to our hair and horns, and we will carry you over the mountains.'

The Pekinese eagerly helped each other to mount the shaggy creatures, until all were safely seated and holding on. Then the goats started off, the one carrying Amber Face leading the way, the others following in single file, each with a Pekinese warrior between his horns.

The sun rode high in the sky, now cleared of rain clouds, as they wound their way up, up, up over the rocks. Sometimes one of the surefooted creatures would stumble. Once, he who had Chu upon his back lost his footing for several paces and slid with a shower of rocks down a perilous slope.

'Do not fear, Pekinese warrior,' he said kindly, when he had regained the path, 'no goat slips for long.'

Sometimes they crossed narrow chasms between the rocks, leaping several feet, and the Pekinese shut their eyes and trembled. For they were not a mountain race. Up and up they went, until they could see the sun glinting gold and silver upon the great snowy peaks above them. The stark white paradise hurt their eyes to look upon and snatched away their speech with its beauty. And after many hours they began to drop down again, over the boulders and rushing streams to the trees and grass of the foothills. It was evening time when at last the goats, descending on to a grassy pasture, put down their riders. At once a flock of young and tender goats, not old enough to accompany their parents, gathered around to greet them.

Amber Face and Chu opened their pouches and handed out presents, tiny collars of gold and little shoes, and silver bells. These the young goats put on, and skipped with pleasure to hear them tinkle.

But the warriors, eager to go on, waited only to thank their kind steeds, and set off down the slopes to the darkening valley.

10. The Distressed Dragon

That night they camped on the very edge of the deep and gloomy forest where their enemies lived. Amber Face looked yet again at his jade dragon, saw that in its green depths the colour glowed brightly, and knew that Stars in a Dark Pool was still alive and well. This he told Chu-i.

'As the Princess is still well,' said Chu, 'would it not be wise to halt here and prepare ourselves to meet the monkeys?'

'On the plain,' agreed his friend, 'we can make spears and shields and the other things we need, without fear of attack from those who haunt the darknesses.'

'Let us then spend this day in cutting weapons, collecting food and making our plans,' suggested Chu.

So Amber Face called to the warriors, who were drinking from a nearby stream after their breakfast, and sent them off four by four to collect wood and sharp stones. Leaving two to guard the camp, Amber Face and Chu trotted off themselves to see what they could find.

'Some beast has been here,' said Chu, snuffing the ground busily as they approached a little hillock.

'Some very large beast,' said Amber Face, looking at a row of five-toed tracks in the mud.

'Walk warily, O Amber Face,' said Chu. 'Maybe it is an enemy.'

And they shuffled cautiously up the side of the hillock.

'What is that noise I hear?' said Amber Face, his ear cocked.

'As if from the depths of the earth,' added Chu, listening.

'It sounds like somebody in distress.'

Rather faintly from the middle of the hillock rose up a slow, wailing sob, and then another and another. Then there was a snorting and a shuffling and a flapping noise beneath them, and a groan and an angry growl. Then more sobs, as whatever it was gave up the struggle and subsided.

'Who are you?' shouted Amber Face, his majestic nose laid flat on the earth. But only fresh sobs answered him. So the two Pekinese crept carefully up the hillock on their stomachs, their tails low, and peered over the edge. At its base was an old badger-hole, and before the badger-hole was stretched out a green, scaly animal, wriggling and pulling and flapping its great wings.

'Inside the badger-hole,' said Chu wisely, 'there must be a head to this animal.'

They scampered down the bank and stood one each side of the dragon's neck.

'How did you get in?' shouted Amber Face. But the dragon, which was evidently a baby one, only sobbed.

'If you will only listen,' said Chu, giving it a sharp nip on the neck where its scales were still tender, 'we may be able to help you!'

At this the dragon stopped its groans and sighs and grunted. By putting their ears close, they could just hear it.

'I am stuck,' it said.

'This dragon is not old enough to be out alone,' said Amber Face. 'But I will call the rest, and we will scratch until it is free.'

So he yapped his gathering cry, and the eight Pekinese came up from the skirts of the wood.

'Keep still inside there,' shouted Chu, 'and we will dig until you are free.'

So they ranged themselves round the hole, five a side, and scratched with their feathery paws, their tails bobbing like chrysanthemums. They dug and dug and scraped and cleared the earth, snuffling and panting. And all the time the baby dragon groaned and tugged at his inconvenient head and

flapped his wings so fiercely that two of the warriors were blown over.

'Keep still,' bellowed Amber Face, 'you are nearly free.'

Then another scratch and a long tug, and the beast pulled its head clear, scattering showers of mud and pebbles over its rescuers. And with its head came a crowd of angry buzzing bees.

But at this moment there was a great whirring of wings overhead, and a shadow between them and the sun, and a huge mother dragon swooped down, hissing angrily and waving her tail.

'Who is molesting my child?' she screamed, and the warriors were obliged to scramble behind the hillock to avoid the great streams of fire that she blew out from her nostrils. As it was, the whiskers of the amber faced were singed, and the ruff of one of his warriors almost set alight.

But when she understood what had happened, and when she saw the sign of the five-toed Imperial dragon spread on the warriors' doublets, she thanked them, and turned her rage upon the young dragon. He was sitting near the hole, trying to lick the mud off his nose, and to soothe the bee stings which had penetrated the soft armour of his face.

'Bad and greedy animal,' said his mother, washing him with her tongue. 'He who runs away to look for honey can expect nothing better than to get stuck.'

'I could not reach the honey,' said the poor dragon, forlornly.

'And a good thing, too,' buzzed the angry queen bee, who had settled on the young dragon's nose again.

'What does your son mean by marauding our nest in this way?' she continued, hovering over his mother. 'What are we going to feed upon, if other people eat our honey?'

'I am indeed sorry for the habits of my foolish son,' said the widow dragon unhappily. 'Again and again I have warned him not to put his head in at people's doors in that sudden manner.' And she sighed deeply.

'And to talk of doors,' said the queen, buzzing angrily up to where the Pekinese were ranged along the hillock, peering over, 'Look at *our* door! Look what you have done to it! There might have been a volcano near at hand!'

'Almost,' said Amber Face, smiling, 'there was. But I would remind you, excellent lady of sweet flowers, who feeds upon nectar, that you could neither have come in nor gone out of your door while it was full of dragon.' And he bowed very low. 'But we will, if it would please you, replace the earth.'

And they set about digging it back the other way. When the bees were busy coming and going again, the mother dragon heaved a deep sigh and said —

'Is there anything that a dragon can do, unhappy and un-skilled as she is, to help the Imperial Pekinese warriors whose kingdom her relations guard so jealously?'

'You might help us collect wood for weapons,' said Amber face doubtfully, and he explained what they were doing here on the edge of the forest.

When she heard of the monkeys, the dragon was full of concern for the gallant Pekinese, so small and so brave. And being a sentimental animal, she hated to think of the faithful Amber Face disappointed of his beautiful bride. So she burnt off strong sticks for them with her breath and sharpened them with her claws; and she peeled off a dozen of her thick-est and oldest scales and gave them to the warriors for breast-plates. She sent her son off to dig out sharp stones from the rocks, and these they fastened to some of the sticks to make spears. She lit their fire and cooked their meal with her fiery breath, and even gave them some of it to carry with them, in a firepot, so that they should never lack warmth in the dank forest. Then she called to her son (who was eating the titbits left over from their meal) – 'Come quickly, Five-toed and Foolish, we have a long way to fly before nightfall.'

And the warriors stood up to wave to them as they flew away on creaking wings. Then they collected their weapons and fastened on their leathery breastplates and prepared to enter the forest. A bright blue magpie with coral-red bill and feet swung upon the bamboo stalks, watching the warriors with eager eyes. Amber Face kow-towed —

'Where in this forest,' he said politely, 'do the monkeys dwell, whose leader has a crooked thumb on his left hand?'

'They passed this way but two days ago,' said the magpie, 'carrying two like yourselves in a bamboo chair. Go on and go on till the end of the forest glimmers and there you may find them. But I, while they camped here, I stole the pretty silver key which opened the ladies' chair! Ha ha he!' laughed the magpie.

'But that key,' said Amber Face eagerly, 'would be of the

greatest value to me. For they have stolen the ladies away, and we go to fetch them back.'

'What will you give me for the key?'

'Would a pearl ring do?' said the warrior.

'Bring it to my bill and I will see.'

So the warrior drew out the ring he had brought for Stars in a Dark Pool, and held it up. Then the magpie hopped to a hollow branch and came fluttering back with the little silver key, which he laid in Amber Face's paw. And he left him the pearl ring, too, for love of the bright eyes of the Pekinese lady in the chair.

11. The Sacred Leopard

Amber Face fastened the little silver key on a strong piece of creeper under his ruff, and the warriors went forward joyfully into the forest, pleased to have heard some news of the monkeys at last.

'Make us a song, O Chu, that we can sing in the green gloom,' they said.

So Chu thought for a while and then sang a song about their adventures, so that they should learn it and remember their good fortune.

THE SONG OF THE JOURNEY
There was a cormorant sat in a boat
(By all the gods of wall and moat)
He carried us up the river afloat
And gave us dainty fish to eat
(Worship the gods of wall and moat
And Madame Wind, who blew our boat).

There was a turtle sat on a bank
(He knew our ancestors of rank)
He dived to the depths of the river dank
To look for the dragon, where it had sunk.
And the fish who the little jade dragon had drunk
Spewed it out safe: so the gods we thank.

There was a wizard dwelt in a cave
(The Master of the Rain did rave)
He gave us shelter and counsel brave
He spelt us riddles we could not solve
(The Master of the Rain shall have
Worship, who sent us to the cave).

There were twelve goats on the mountain-side
(Praise to the Lady who sweeps the Sky)
And over the snows we were safely led
For on their backs the rocks we rid
(The Lady who sweeps the Sky so wide
Showed the way on the mountain-side).

There was a dragon stuck by his jaws
(Praise to the dragons who guard our doors)
We helped the young with merciful paws
And his mother repaid with scales and claws.
(The dragons who guard the Imperial doors
Keep us safe in evil hours).

There was a magpie sat on a tree
(Praise to the Heavenly Beings three)
Who stole for us the silver key
And through the forest told us the way.
(Praise to the Heavenly Beings three
And the peaches of Immortality).

The warriors, delighted with this song, sang it as they trod the undergrowth, and at first felt only grateful for dangers overcome. But as they sang, pride crept into their swelling hearts and they kept their jaws high in the air, and their chests puffed up before them. So it happened that they did not see a meagre member of the despicable race of the snakes which reared its head from the bushes by the path.

The snake grew envious as he listened and gathering his venom, he slid down and bit the last of the brave band as it passed him.

Poor Amber Face, walking last, received the bite on his leg, and quick as thought plunged into the undergrowth to kill the beast. But it had slid quietly away, and not so much as a rustle betrayed it.

'Stop, O Chu, stop singing, O Pekinese,' said the Mandarin, for the others had not seen him fall behind. 'There is a snake in the bushes, and it has wounded me on the leg.' And he moaned with fright.

The distressed Pekinese gathered round their leader.

'Where is the poisonous beast?' said Chu-i.

'It has slid away,' said Amber Face faintly, as he sickened from the bite.

And Chu sent off two warriors to scour the ground for the monster.

'But take care, O Pekinese, for his colour is as the colour of the ground.'

'And you two,' said the faithful Chu, 'search quickly in the streams and holes for the two-coloured leeches.'

And two more ran quickly to find healing leaves; and four cut branches and twigs and wove them into a hammock for the wounded Mandarin. But the two bravest Chu sent to the forest depths to find out if there were, by any chance, a sacred leopard dwelling there, spotted and silken; and to see if they could by any means persuade him to give them the fat of his leg to anoint their master.

Chu-i himself stayed near at hand to cherish his friend. Choosing a space cleared of undergrowth, and close to a stream, they slung the hammock between two low branches to lift him off the damp earth. And Chu applied leeches to his wound to suck the poison, and tended him carefully as a mother. Opening the little bottle made of a single chrysoprase, he took three pinches of the shredded rhinoceros horn, and dissolving it in sweet juice, gave it to the warrior to drink in an egg-shell. But Amber Face tossed and turned restlessly on his hammock, and groaned with the pain of his leg, and as the day drew on passed first to unconsciouness and then to stillness, lying as if he were dead already.

'Keep the fire bright and warm,' ordered Chu of the two Pekinese who tended it, 'and I will go and call into the forest in case those who went to seek the leopard are close by.'

So they gathered more sticks and made tea of fresh green leaves over the flames, to give to Amber Face, who still lay like a log, with foam at his mouth. The day was drawing in, when Chu, who was crouched low over the fire weeping softly into his paws, sprang to his feet and listened intently.

'Do you hear anything, O Chu?' said one of the sorrowing band.

'The crackle of footfalls in the far distance,' said Chu, 'and it is not only two Pekinese who come.'

As they listened they heard the soft patter of four Pekinese feet approaching, but behind them the slower pad, pad of a larger beast, walking on its fours.

'The leopard! The leopard!' rejoiced the warriors; and one ran to the hammock to look at their leader, and another made ready bandages of leaves, and Chu stood silently by the fire watching the bushes. The footsteps came nearer until they were at hand. Then the two Pekinese appeared through the low twigs. And above them, staring into the clearing through the bushes, was the green-eyed, spotted leopard.

Now, often at other times the leopard had hunted with the Pekinese, emerging from his forests to join them in the chase. When he heard of their distress he admired their gallantry and had allowed himself to be led to the spot where Amber

Face lay. With him he brought a little hollow gourd, in which was the fat from his sacred leg.

'O friendly leopard. O kind and sacred animal,' said Chu, kow-towing, and almost dead with watching.

'Where is the little warrior?' asked the leopard kindly. And he walked over to the hammock, skirting the fire with side-long glances, and warmed him with his breath.

'Anoint his leg with the oil from the gourd,' he said, 'and be quick, for he draws breath but faintly.'

Then they melted the contents of the gourd over the fire and cleansed it and put it on the wound, binding it with leaves. And soon, while they all stood watching, the warrior's breath began to rise and fall regularly, and they knew that he was lapped in a peaceful sleep. The grateful Pekinese fell at the leopard's feet and said their thanks.

'What can we do,' said Chu, 'to repay you for your kindness?'

'I will share your fire for the night, little Mandarin,' replied the leopard, 'and you shall tell me all your adventures.'

So they flung themselves down round the fire, and the Pekinese, hungry from a long fast, ate and drank, while the spotted leopard lay further off, contented in the blaze, and licked his hind leg, for it was sore at the spot where he had taken the fat.

While one watched over the sick warrior, the rest told the leopard of their adventures, and how they were come to the very threshold of the monkeys' home.

'They are a mean and spiteful race,' said he, 'and none is cunning save Wang their king. But how are you going to win back the ladies, you so few and so small, and far from home, and they in a forest that they know?' and he yawned a great, wide-open yawn.

'We have made plans,' said Chu, 'that while we attack from the front and engage them in fight, Amber Face shall steal round to their stronghold and see if he can free the

He yawned a great, wide-open yawn

Princess. For we have the key to her chair.'

'But the amber-faced warrior will not be fit for this for several days,' remarked the leopard.

'We shall wait here and learn the forest paths and the ways of escape, until he is well,' replied Chu-i.

And the leopard yawned again and growled slightly in his throat, but said nothing.

One by one the Pekinese, worn out with anxiety, fell asleep, except one warrior who watched over their leader.

When they awoke in the morning, the sacred leopard was gone, and only the marks of his claws in the earth where he had stretched and scratched showed that he had been there at all.

12. The Little Bamboo Chair

The amber-faced warrior awoke deliciously and weakly out of his long sleep, to hear subdued voices talking near at hand.

'We have been, O Chui-i,' two of the Pekinese were saying, 'right up to the edge of the hollow where the villains live.'

'And where is this hollow, and how many leagues away?' replied Chu's voice.

'It lies at the other side of the forest. On this side of it is a steep slope, and on the other, open and rocky land, free of trees.'

'But how did you go so near without disturbing their guards?' said another.

'We saw no guards watching on top of the slope,' replied the warriors.

'And what were the monkeys doing?'

'Sitting in their separate trees on branches which hang opposite the top of the slope,' they said.

'If, then, we were to steal up from the forest —' said Chu-i.

'And shoot arrows down from above —' said another.

'And charge down the slopes —' said a third.

'Driving them out of the forest —' said a fourth.

'We might keep them employed while the amber-faced warrior rescues his lady!' said Chu-i.

And by this time their voices were grown loud with excitement, and Amber Face could hear their paws as they pattered and jumped on the leaves and sticks of the forest floor.

'O would that the amber warrior were well!' sighed Chu.

And at this, Amber Face, still drowsy and weak, roused

himself and said —

'I am awake, O Pekinese, and I have heard your talk!'

In a moment the whole band were gathered round the hammock, yickering and whining with pleasure to hear their leader speak. One brought hot tea, and another a piece of a fish they had caught in the stream and had roasted over the

fire. Soon Amber Face sat propped in his hammock, his wound cleansed and newly dressed, sipping his tea, while they talked of the way they would rout the monkeys. And as he sipped and listened, the amber-faced warrior remembered a strange dream.

'Chu-i, and my brave warriors,' he began. 'I have dreamt a dream while I slept. The spotted leopard came to me and anointed my wound with the oil from his sacred leg.'

The warriors looked from one to the other, and shook their whiskers.

'This was no dream,' said Chu gently, 'for he came indeed,

and saved your life when we all despaired.'

'And how long did he stay?' asked the puzzled warrior.

'He shared our fire, but when we awoke he was gone.'

'There was more to my dream,' said Amber Face. 'Before he went he came to me again, and told me to take courage; and if in our battle with the monkeys we were in distress, we should call upon him by a name, and he would come.'

'And what was the name?' they asked eagerly.

'That I cannot remember,' replied the warrior, frowning.

'Think no more of it now,' said Chu wisely. 'And some moment when you are at rest it will float into your mind and be there, like a lotus on the water.'

Amber Face grew hourly stronger, and soon was on his feet again with the rest, helping to prepare for the attack. A few days later, when he was well and his wound healed, and all was ready, the Pekinese arose long before dawn, donned their breast-plates, picked up their spears and arrows, and set out in single file, the two who knew the way leading them. One held the fire-pot, born of the dragon's breath, and from this they lit torches to see their way.

As they trod the forest, Amber Face heard suddenly in his mind the voice of the leopard, soft and velvety, as clear as if he were at hand. 'Call upon me as the Spotted Supple One, and I will come.' And he was glad, and told the rest.

It was that hour before light, and the colours of things were not yet born in the forest around them, when they approached the edge of the hollow in which the monkeys lived. Here the Pekinese who led the way halted.

'Tread gently from now on, O warriors,' they whispered, 'for we are nearing the end of our journey.'

And Amber Face, while they halted, looked at the jade dragon in his pouch. He was dismayed to see that by the growing pearly light the dragon looked paler.

'Let us hurry, O warriors,' he said, showing it to the rest, 'for the Princess grows faint with waiting. Here we will wish

Here Amber Face left them

each other blessings and success. And by the Jade Emperor, may I find the Princess quickly!'

'By Kuan-ti, may we hold the tribe in fight, while you loose the prisoners!' added Chu-i.

'By the gods of the hearth, may we see our homes again,' added the rest.

And they said no goodbyes to each other.

Then they crept onward until they lay stomachs to the ground, peering into the hollow. Here Amber Face left them, each with his arrow aimed at one of the huddled figures still sleeping in the trees opposite.

'Forget not the name of the sacred leopard,' he whispered, 'and give me a little time.'

They nodded, and Amber Face turned away, wondering as he skirted the edge of the hollow when he would see any of his gallant friends again.

When he found himself looking down upon a patch of

thick bushes which lay between him and the trees of the sleeping monkeys, he began to descend the slope. Cautiously, step by step, he snuffled along, until he could hide in the shade of the green laurels and camellias. From one of these bright bushes covered with waxy scarlet flowers he picked two blossoms, and put them in his pouch for the Princess and her maid. Just before dawn he emerged into the bottom of the hollow and saw, not far off, perched upon a small rock, the little bamboo chair! Hardly able to contain himself for joy, he scrambled up the crag and fumbled for the silver key round his neck. Then he tapped gently and whispered.

'Do not be alarmed. It is I, Amber Face!'

And he opened the door and went in.

Golden Bells gave a little yelp of fright and pleasure, but Stars in a Dark Pool, exhausted by fears and trials, could only open her starry eyes wide and fall into the Mandarin's paws, shivering with excitement.

At this moment there was a curious whizzing in the air, followed by shrieks and yelps, and the sound of branches breaking, and then more arrows hissing, and a confused scrambling noise as the alarmed and wounded monkeys, taken by surprise before they were awake, flung themselves to the ground.

'What is it, O what is it?' said Stars in a Dark Pool, clutching the warrior.

'It is the Pekinese from the forest above, attacking the monkeys,' said he.

And then they heard a crashing and roaring and yapping and tumbling as the gallant band, having dislodged their enemies from the branches, swept down the slope against them.

'Make ready to run with me,' said the warrior, 'for as soon as it is safe we are to escape.'

13. The Battle and the Eagle

Meanwhile, as Chu had hoped, the monkeys, thinking such a shower of weapons must have come from many more than eleven warriors, had dashed for the open spaces beyond the forest. Here the Pekinese followed them, chanting their battle song, flinging sharp stones and poisoned spears, shooting their arrows thick and fast. The monkeys, having had no time to collect weapons, could fight only with stones, but by degrees they collected themselves into a band and turned on the Pekinese. Pitching down great boulders, flinging showers of pebbles, they fought desperately for the forest again, knowing that once near the trees they could both escape from and probably defeat the Pekinese.

Back and back the Pekinese retreated, dodging the stones, shooting their lessening arrows sparingly. On came the monkeys, nearer and nearer, with cries and yells.

'O Spotted Supple One,' cried Chu-i, in despair, 'help us!'

And there was a great roar and a streak of fawn, and a flash of spots as the sacred animal leapt from behind a rock, sheer upon the oncoming line of Wang's band. Encouraged by his presence, the Pekinese surged forward again, seized the monkeys by the heels and bit their tails and arms.

'Curs and cowards,' said the watchful Wang, as careful as cunning, when he saw that no more hope was left to them, who had incurred the wrath of the terror of the forest. And immediately he thought of the Princess, and how best he could harm her and fulfil his revenge. He leapt to a high rock where an eagle sat, looking down on the battle and awaiting her prey.

'All the corpses shall you have, O fierce-beaked bird, if you

A great roar and a streak of fawn and a flash of spots

will but pick up the bamboo chair which stands in the hollow and carry it to the most inaccessible peak on the furthest mountain.'

And the eagle fluttered up and away, and hovered, and then swooped down into the forest.

Then Wang called off as many of his band as could still run and swing.

'The trees, O brave ones,' he shouted. 'No hope is left but the high trees. Look to your Princess, little yellow people,' he jeered, 'she will soon be beyond your reach.' And he raced and swung himself high into a tree, and those who could follow, followed, wondering at his words.

At this the leopard ceased from his labours, and the Pekinese, panting, looked with alarm into the air, where the wicked monkey pointed. As they watched, the great golden eagle rose from the forest carrying in her claws the bamboo chair. They could just see the faces of the amber warrior, Golden Bells and the Princess looking fearfully out of the window.

The warriors turned pale beneath their fur.

'O Chu-i, O sacred leopard,' they wailed, 'it is all in vain that we came!'

'The warrior and his Princess and the faithful Golden Bells – all lost!' said Chu miserably.

'What shall we do? What shall we do?' all echoed. And they turned to the sacred spotted one standing close at hand. But the leopard, for once, was at a loss.

'There is nothing that we can do,' he replied sadly. 'For no Pekinese could attempt those high rocks.'

'Let us follow and try,' said one.

'But we cannot see where they have gone,' said another. For by this time the eagle and the chair were out of sight in the next range of mountains.

'He! He! He!' chittered the monkeys from the edge of the forest. And the leopard turned angrily and growled, which silenced them.

'There is but one thing I can do,' he said, 'and that is to see you, O Chu-i, and your gallant band back to your Imperial kingdom, so that you are not molested by certain folk on the way,' and he cast a glance backwards at the forest.

'As for the valiant amber warrior,' he continued, seeing the Pekinese crestfallen and uncertain, 'if there is a way of escape from his present unenviable position, he will find it.'

'You are right, sacred animal,' said Chu-i sadly, looking at his friends who had come through so many dangers, and then at the gloomy forest. 'We must trust to the Jade Emperor and the Imperial dragons who guard us to help our Prince.'

Then the sacred leopard attended to their wounds, licked them and bound them up. And, after resting for half the day, and eating a meal, they turned silently back into the forest, Chu-i leading the way and the leopard guarding the rear.

Not long afterwards a mighty storm burst over the mountains behind them, and the rain battered upon the forest trees until they were deafened by its roar.

'O Amber Face!' they muttered, thinking of their three friends and wondering what had befallen them.

'Let us hope,' said Chu-i, 'that they will find their way down from the heights again.' But secretly in his heart he was afraid that they had been dashed to pieces on the rocks by the treacherous eagle.

And each Pekinese thought likewise, but said nothing. And all prayed for the safety of the three in the mountains.

It was weary going, even though they were heading for home; for they had not the heart to sing, and each felt guilty as he caught himself thinking with pleasure of his own hearth and his father's house, when the Prince and Princess and the faithful Golden Bells were so far from any comfort. The leopard showed them shorter ways through forest and over mountain, for he knew the paths of this country well. When they lit their fire at night he would lie, not in their circle with them, but sprawled a leopard's length or two away. Sometimes he would disappear for a while. The Pekinese took no notice of this, for they had never gone far before they would hear again the pad of his feet behind them. And they asked no questions.

But when they came out at last on to the broad plain and had crossed the river, and knew that only a day's march

in the open lay between them and their kingdom, the sacred beast came quietly up to Chu-i, who headed the band, and said gently —

'Here, little Mandarin, I will leave you, for my haunts lie behind me, and are not in open country.'

'Will you not come to our kingdom, to receive the thanks of our Emperor?' said Chu-i.

'I will go back whence I came,' repeated the leopard, 'but if I should hear aught of the little amber-faced one and his ladies, I will give them my help.'

So the Pekinese kow-towed, thanking the sacred animal, their hearts full of longing for the amber warrior. And the leopard purred softly and left them.

The warriors turned away heavy-hearted, and walked on in silence, wondering in their puzzled minds what they should tell the Emperor and the War Lords and the waiting Pekinese when they reached their kingdom.

14. Thunder and Lightning

As for the amber-faced warrior, he and the two Pekinese ladies had been on the point of stealing from the chair into the forest while the battle was at its thickest, when suddenly they were aware of a curious sensation. The chair began to rise from the rock with a gentle swinging motion.

'Help! O help!' said Stars in a Dark Pool, 'we are caught again.'

'Open the door quickly,' said Golden Bells, 'and let us escape!'

But so quickly had they been carried that it was already too late to scramble out. Amber Face looked with alarm from the window to see that the rock was some feet below them, and that they were quickly approaching the tips of the forest trees.

'O fool that I am!' he wailed. 'Why was I not more watchful? It is too late now to jump.'

'Who is carrying us?' asked the Princess, in fear.

'I can hear wings,' said her maid. 'It must be some great bird.'

And as they listened they heard the regular flap, flap of whirring wings above them.

'At least our brave friends are safe,' said the warrior, as they peered out over the battlefield and saw the Pekinese and the sacred leopard staring unhappily after them.

'Who is it who has joined them?' asked the Princess in an awed whisper.

'It is the Spotted Supple One,' replied Amber Face; and he told them the story of his wounded leg. This tale threw the Princess into alarm, and she examined the warrior's leg to make sure that no poison remained in it.

Amber Face continued to talk cheerfully to them, while keeping a watch out of the window of the chair.

'After all,' he thought to himself, 'if we are to be dashed to pieces on the rocks, or starved to death in the mountains, at least we die together.'

But he said nothing to the two bright-eyed damsels, who sat trustfully watching him, seeming to feel that all was well if he were with them.

Up and up they soared, and through a soft bank of low white cloud, and past rocks and crags and precipices which made the warrior tremble, though he hid his fear from the others.

'Tell me, O Golden Bells,' said he, 'how much food and drink we have with us in the chair.'

Golden Bells looked under one of the tiny seats.

'Only a little rice and a little meat,' she replied, 'left over from yesterday, and one little sweet cake, and about six egg-shells full of milk; for the monkeys used to bring us our food in the morning.'

This was a serious matter. For though the warrior had begun to hope that the bird did not intend to drop them (for what was the point in this case of carrying them so far?), yet he realised that their fate might be even worse if they were to be left deserted on a rocky crag.

At this moment, even as he feared, their long flight was over and the chair came to rest on something solid. The great bird hovered near the window and looked in at them.

'Have mercy and do not leave us here,' said Amber Face in terror, 'we have never wronged you or your kind!'

But the spiteful eagle merely laughed into her tawny wings and fluttered off, the way she had come.

'What is the matter, O Amber Face?' asked the Princess. 'Can we not now leave our prison and escape?'

Poor Princess! She had not seen, as he had, the long, steep flight into the mountains. But as she and Golden Bells peeped over the Mandarin's shoulders and looked out on the empty air and the crags around, and the deep, deep precipice beneath, they shrieked and fainted away with terror.

Amber Face revived them with milk, holding the trembling Princess in his arms. 'Do not fear,' said he kindly, 'for if there is a way to escape, we will find it. O, Golden Bells, comfort your mistress while I look out and see our position.'

And he put his head from the window, and saw that they were resting on a narrow ledge of rock underneath an overhanging crag on the very top of the world. Snow-covered peaks glistened in the distance, and the steeps that he could see were bare of any gentle mantling of green. Lonely and loveless lay the bare mountains. The warrior called from the window, though without hope.

'Help, help, help!'

Plaintively the echo answered once, twice, thrice round the slopes, 'Help, help, help!'

His heart beat fast with panic at the mysterious answer, and his head reeled with the silence and the heights. There was nothing to be done, but keep up their spirits as best he could. So he turned back as cheerfully as possible, ate a little of the food which Golden Bells had prepared, and entertained the two downcast maidens with stories of their journey.

It was still early in the morning, but the sun, red and glowering, was hidden behind a curtain of cloud, which seemed, as they sat, to come closer and closer. Darker and darker grew the sky, and the hours seemed longer and longer. The Princess and her maid fell asleep, but no sleep came to the watchful Mandarin, who sat with his eyes upon the distant slopes. Gradually the rain mist hid them from his sight, and the clouds rolled and lolled around until even the nearby rocks were strange dim shapes, brooding as if they were the silence itself.

Then the lightning split the sky, jagged and angry and beautiful.

'It is only the Mother of Lightnings, who chastises our enemies,' said Amber Face to himself.

Then the thunder rocked and roared and hurtled its great hollow cubes over the heavens.

'It is only my Lord the Thunder,' said Amber Face to the ladies who awoke startled, 'casting his bolts at our enemies.'

Then came the rain, hissing and battering on the rocks and on the roof of the chair.

'It is only the Master of the Rain, who sends us drink,' said the warrior; and he held out a little cup which was soon full of fresh water.

And the storm continued with violent force for a long while. After an hour or so the rain lessened, and the lightning called back her shafts, and the Lord of the Thunder went to attend to business elsewhere, leaving only the little Thunders playing at hide and seek in the heavens. And Amber Face pulled out the jade dragon and prayed fervently and bid the others do so too.

As the rain ceased, they could distinguish a steady drip, drip, drip upon their roof. At first they took no notice of this, thinking that a swollen gully was overflowing from the rocks above. But when they heard a sob, and a choking noise, they sat up and listened.

'What is that?' said the Princess, pricking her sharp ears.

The sobs increased and the drips upon the roof fell faster. By this time the rain had stopped, so the warrior put his face out of the window and called, 'Is there anybody there?'

There was silence for a minute, then a shuffling noise, and a head appeared over the crag, its eyes streaming with tears. It was the baby dragon.

'Five-toed and Foolish!' said Amber Face, in glee. 'What brings you here?'

'I have been chased by the little Thunders,' he sobbed, 'and my coat is wet and I have lost my mother in the mist.'

The Princess leant out of the chair and passed him a handkerchief

'This is good fortune indeed!' said Amber Face. 'For your worthy mother will certainly not cease looking until she finds you, and if you will only stay here, perhaps she will find us too.'

'Where is the poor animal?' said the Princess, who had a tender heart. And she leant out of the chair and passed him

a handkerchief. The five-toed one dried his eyes, shook the rain off his wings, and was soon smiling happily, as he munched the little sweet cake provided by Golden Bells, and boasted of his perilous flight.

Very soon the Lady who Sweeps the Sky Clear came with her broom and hustled the clouds away. Through the parting mist they heard a creaking of wings and an anxious voice drawing nearer and nearer.

'Five-toed and Green-coated! Where are you? It is I, your loving mother!'

The dragon raised himself carefully on his front claws and waved the Princess's handkerchief from his mouth.

'O, you bad and disobedient animal!' she began as she saw him, her anxiety forgotten in her relief.

'Do not blame him,' called Amber Face, 'for his adventure has saved our lives!'

And when the widow had landed on the crag and heard their tale, and seen the frightened Princess and her little maid, she was too interested to blame her son.

'I will carry you to your kingdom,' she said, waddling officiously along the ledge, and looking in at the window, 'and my son shall follow. First, I will pick up the chair, but when we are out of the mountains, you shall ride between my wings, O royal couple!' And she beamed with pleasure.

Then perching again on the crag, she leant down and picked up the chair with her strong claw. Soon they were sailing over the mountains again, the widow dragon calling every moment to her son to keep close.

15. Happiness

The Pekinese were keeping a festival inside their kingdom. Since early dawn they had been preparing offerings for their ancestors, each in his family, the father hurrying hither and thither with candles and incense, the mother bringing the white moon cakes or fruit or flowers to lay before the tablet of father and grandfather. It was a bright summer day, and when their oblations were over, they would be seen in the streets and gardens, basking in the sunshine, listening to the military music, or floating gently along the rivers in their boats.

The Emperor himself, prostrate in the Temple of Ancestors in the palace, lit candles and burnt incense sticks, offered a moon cake and mulberries, and praying protection for his lost daughter and her rescuers, betook himself to his favourite spot in the Imperial gardens. Here, he lay beneath a mulberry tree near the edge of a lake where a peacock strutted and mandarin ducks sailed on the water, and a brilliant kingfisher perched on a pink peony.

In this place the Official of the Court found him some time later, dreaming into the untroubled pool. Fussily he approached, kow-towing at every step, and peered between the low hanging mulberry leaves to see if the Emperor was asleep.

'A messenger has come, beloved of the Lord of Heaven, from the Imperial gateway,' he began.

'Let him approach,' said the Emperor.

'He has given me his message, and I have sent him away,' replied Tu Fu.

'What is his message?' asked the Emperor.

The old Official, fussy and officious, kow-towed three times more and said —

'It is a message of some importance. The guards on the wall imagine that they have discerned on the distant horizon an approaching band of Pekinese, doubtless the warriors returning triumphant with the Princess.'

And he bowed again.

The Emperor leapt to his feet with a growl of surprise, left the old man bowing at the mulberry tree, and trotted as fast as he could go to the palace.

'The Emperor's palanquin!' called the servants. And in a very short while he was on the wall, straining his eyes to see the speck of dust in the distance, which was the returning band.

Soon he was joined by the illustrious General Puffer, father of the amber-faced warrior, and his other war-lord, General Snorter.

'What is this we hear, O Imperial Majesty?' said they, scrambling up the steps to the top of the broad wall.

'I was summoned by a toad,' whispered General Snorter behind his hand, 'from the very tablet of my ancestors.'

The Emperor simply pointed with his paw, following the direction in which the guard was looking. By this time they could discern quite clearly the movement of the approaching Pekinese.

'I can see no chair or palanquin,' said the Emperor with a

puzzled frown, a few minutes later, 'such as ladies would travel in.'

'It seems to me,' said General Puffer anxiously, 'that they hold their standards down, which is no way for a victorious expedition to return.'

'I cannot see very well,' quavered old Tu Fu who had joined them, 'but I think the party is too small for fourteen.' And he adjusted his spectacles and peered uneasily through them.

And in a little while, as the figures grew more and more distinct, they began to count.

'One – two – three – four – five – six,' muttered the Generals, 'seven – eight – nine – ten – eleven —'

'I see no more than eleven,' said the Emperor. 'By all the musical stones,' he said, 'who is it who is missing?'

Nearer and nearer they came, and now there was no mistaking their attitude of dejection.

'Who leads the band?' said one.

'I think it is Chu-i,' replied another.

'And he in the rear is not Amber Face,' sighed the Emperor. 'Something is amiss,' he said, turning to go down. And the rest followed; all except General Puffer, who gazed sadly at each trotting warrior in turn, trying to believe that one of them was his son.

The returning Pekinese were soon inside the gates, exhausted with their journey, and able only to shake their heads miserably at the questions of the crowd around them.

'What has happened, O Chu-i,' said the Emperor in anguish, 'to my daughter, Stars in a Dark Pool, the loveliest lady in the kingdom?'

And all the Pekinese groaned and whined and snuffled with distress.

'And what of my son?' said poor General Puffer, quietly, from the edge of the crowd.

And Chu-i, after some refreshment, told his story, kneeling before the Emperor, the Pekinese squatting all round in widening circles. All differences of rank were forgotten, so enthralled were they; and the Emperor, the Generals and the crowd wept together as Chu-i described the disappearance of the three brave Pekinese in the chair.

'There is still hope,' said Chu-i, 'that the eagle did but place them on some high rock, from which the resourceful warrior will escape.'

'It is more likely,' said the Emperor filled with gloom, 'that they have been dashed to pieces in the mountains and we shall never see them alive.'

'The curses of hell upon the monkeys!' they cried.

And so low were their heads bowed, so loud was the sobbing in the city, that they did not see and hear the strange apparition which the guards upon the wall were watching.

'Look up! Look up,' cried the guards, 'for something approaches from the air and we have no power to stop it!'

The Pekinese to a man forgot their sorrow and gazed up into the sky. Two green dragons had flown out of the west and were nearing the kingdom, the smaller one carrying a little chair in his claws. They circled three times over the crowded city, and then descended in a slow spiral into the market place. And the amber-faced warrior himself, with the beautiful lady Stars in a Dark Pool, clambered off the back of the widow dragon, while out of the little chair which her son placed gently on the ground, stepped the lady Golden Bells.

Amazement kept the Pekinese rooted to the spot, but when Amber Face approached the Emperor, modestly leading the

Princess by the hand, they surged forward, yapping and cheering and dancing round in delighted circles.

'You have done bravely indeed,' said he, 'to escape from the craggy mountains!'

'O, my friend,' cried Chu-i, dancing with excitement, 'little did we think to see you again!' And he embraced the amber warrior with great joy and relief.

Meanwhile, the widow dragon stood demurely in the market place where she had landed, whispering to her son to keep still, and trying to look as if her part in the affair were a mere trifle. But soon Amber Face led the Emperor and his father up to her, and said —

'Here is she who saved our lives, who has fed and cared for us as we journeyed home.'

And he told the whole story.

The widow blushed and curtsied as she received their thanks, and an invitation to the wedding.

'What I have done was little enough,' she said, 'and your thanks are mostly due to my foolish son, who contrived to lose himself in the mountains,' and she turned, smiling, towards him. But the Five-toed and Foolish One was in the far corner of the market place, playing at giving rides to a group of adventurous child Pekinese.

And so the wedding was celebrated that very day, with glee and thanksgiving.

And Amber Face gave Stars in a Dark Pool the little jade dragon, his talisman on the journey. And the Princess gave him a little chair made of red lacquer, a model of that in which she had travelled, and inside it the figures of herself and her maid.

And the whole kingdom brought them presents; and the Emperor gave all his people sweet cakes and flowers and sugar plums and peacock feathers, and paper lanterns. And they danced and sang late into the night.

But the Lord of Heaven, the merciful Jade Emperor, afraid

lest his darlings should be molested again by their enemies, picked up the kingdom by the four corners of the plain, as in a blanket, and planted it whole upon the mountain in the middle of the world, where the immortals dwell. And the Lady Queen of the West, Si Wang Mu, who keeps the peach tree whereon the Peaches of Immortality grow, came and threw her peaches to the Pekinese.

So they live for ever in the dwelling of the immortals, where the trees bear precious stones, and where garlands of golden bells edge the clouds, and where the two together make such a sweet tinkling music that Amber Face and Chu-i have entirely forgotten the time of their life upon earth.

And the Princess, drinking the clear, pure water of the streams, has quite forgotten the monkeys.

And here Golden Bells has no need to embroider, for real flowers grow on the Princess's dress. And here the little tree grower cultivates immortal blossom on his trees, and the Princess's maidens taste immortal sweetmeats.

But some few Pekinese slipped out from the corners when the Lord of Heaven lifted the kingdom, and landed upon earth again. These are they you see sometimes looking mournful, the corners of their mouths drooping, for they are thinking with longing of their happy kingdom. But when they look bland and smiling, and wriggle their bodies and rotate their tails, then they are remembering it with pleasure.

For to this kingdom among the immortals, with its fine flowers and fruit, goes every Pekinese when he is sleeping.

The King of the
Copper Mountains

PAUL BIEGEL

For more than a thousand years King Mansolain has reigned over the Copper Mountains, but now he is old and tired. To keep his heart beating, he must hear exciting stories.

So one by one the animals of his Kingdom come to tell their tales – the fierce wolf, the chattering squirrel, and the three-headed dragon, breathing fire. The beetle sits close to the King's ear to tell his story while the other animals lie on his beard. Next comes the mighty lion and last of all, the dwarf. He prophesies that the old King *could* live a thousand more years, but only if the Wonder Doctor arrives in time. . .